MEAT ON THE BONE

Brian Stableford's scholarly work includes *New Atlantis: A Narrative History of Scientific Romance* (Wildside Press, 2016), *The Plurality of Imaginary Worlds: The Evolution of French roman scientifique* (Black Coat Press, 2017) and *Tales of Enchantment and Disenchantment: A History of Faerie* (Black Coat Press, 2019). In support of the latter projects he has translated more than a hundred volumes of *roman scientifique* and more than twenty volumes of *contes de fées* into English. He has edited *Decadence and Symbolism: A Showcase Anthology* (Snuggly Books, 2018), and is busy translating more Symbolist and Decadent fiction.

His recent fiction, in the genre of metaphysical fantasy, includes a trilogy of novels set in West Wales, consisting of *Spirits of the Vasty Deep* (2018), *The Insubstantial Pageant* (2018) and *The Truths of Darkness* (2019), published by Snuggly Books; and a trilogy set in Paris and the south of France, consisting of *The Painter of Spirits*, *The Quiet Dead* and *Living with the Dead*, all published by Black Coat Press in 2019; and the futuristic fantasy *The Revelations of Time and Space* (Snuggly Books 2020).

BRIAN STABLEFORD

MEAT ON THE BONE

A POSTMORTAL ROMANCE

THIS IS A SNUGGLY BOOK

ISBN: 978-1-64525-065-4

MEAT
ON THE BONE

1

The first Saturday in March is reckoned by some to be the first Saturday in spring, and it certainly seemed that way to me as I had an extra long salt bath that left me all a-tingle, and then I polished my ribs and skull with a particular vigor. I always looked forward to going to the Palais, even before my afterlife changed, but that day seemed special, and there was an extra click in my step and an extra metaphorical song in my virtual heart.

Even the bulkier species of the Postmortal, let alone Larvae, tend to think of bony folk as existentially challenged, incapable of much in the way of sensuality, but you certainly don't need squishy flesh to experience pleasure. We skellies prefer to believe, in fact, that the various kinds of gross sensuality that are bundled in material flesh only serve to distract attention from the more refined pleasures of virtual flesh. Except, of course, that you have to have bones; Skellies are in no doubt about that. Ghosts go too far to the opposite extreme. There's no moderation without balance, and you can't dance well without equilibrium. To have a happy afterlife you need virtual flesh and real bones. Whatever anybody else thinks, that's the truth. We skellies like to think of ourselves as the ultimate connoisseurs of existence.

Well, we would, wouldn't we? If we really were missing out on something, we'd hardly be likely to let on, especially to ourselves.

On that Saturday, though, I felt a special buzz when I ran the polishing rag around my eye sockets and loaded the toothpaste on to my brush to make the old pegs sparkle. You have to look after your teeth, if you're a skelly. Just because we're second in resistance to post-mortal wear and tear only to ghosts doesn't mean that we're immune to decay. Afterlife is just like life in that regard, so it's said; we begin to die even before transition, and if you want a long and happy afterlife you have to do your best to keep the forces of decay at bay, whether you start with old bones, like the many, or young bones, like the few—like me. Every day, we wake up and thank Almighty Chance that we weren't metamorphosed as zombies, but no one is safe from the ravages of time and remortality, not even ghosts.

Saturday is a big occasion for almost everyone in the neighborhood. We all have our things to do—including the zombies, although we bony folk don't like to enquire too closely about the details of *their* weekend rituals and enterprises. We're not exclusive, mind. Anyone is welcome at the Palais or the Guignol, and even zombies wouldn't be turned away if they wanted to come in. The tolerance is mostly mutual; the vampires who live up in Transylvania Terraces welcome all comers to their fancy dress parties at the Gothic Castle, but we bony folk don't go in for fancy dress much—or any other kind of dress, unless we have a particular reason to cover up—so you'll very rarely see a skelly at those rarefied heights. The Palais de Danse Macabre, is delicately poised, half way up the Big Hill or half way down, depending on your state of mind.

Some of the squishy folk who hang out at the vamps' ball dress up in black body-stockings with skeletons painted on, with skull masks over their squishy faces, but we don't take offense. We take it as compliment. Perhaps they take it as a compliment that we occasionally dress up, although it's very rare indeed for us to put on rubber masks in order to mimic Larvae. There are limits, after all. How people can dance in fancy dress, or any other kind of clothing, is beyond me. And squishy folk in skelly costumes look utterly pathetic by comparison with the real thing. To be honest, though, most fancy dress looks so pathetic by comparison with whatever it's pretending to be that it's hard to understand why vamps like it so much.

We mustn't judge, though. The airs and graces that vamps put on are bound to seem strange to skellies—although, I suppose, lykes probably understand it a little better, just as they obviously sympathize with needing a red fix, at least when the moon's full—but some of our folkways must seem equally strange to them.

Which makes me pause, in fact, to wonder how best to address this text to its possible readers, if any. I'd like to think that it won't just be of interest to skellies, and perhaps not even primarily interesting to skellies. I'd like to think that vamps and lykes might find it interesting, *because* it's written by a skelly rather than in spite of it, because it gives them a little insight into a different way of thinking, a different way of afterlife. But bearing in mind that I might have readers who aren't skellies does create problems, not just in diplomatic terms, but in terms of comprehension. It means that I'll sometimes have to explain things that every skelly already knows, but which the average vamp or lyke might never even have bothered to think about.

And then there are the ghosts, who might, I suppose, be more interested in the particular story I have to tell than anyone else, and are certainly more likely to take offense. We mustn't judge, as I say . . . but I'm only human, and to be fair, ghosts judge all the time. If ghosts weren't so judgmental, in fact, this story would never have happened. So, my ghost readers, if any, might have to make slight allowances.

And then, there's the possibility that I might have Larval readers—that, one way or another, this text might make its way out of the Ghetto. It's not impossible, maybe not even improbable, if it gets published at all—and bearing that idea in mind adds an extra order of magnitude to the problems of diplomacy and the problems of explanation.

So I'd like to appeal to my readers—all my potential readers—to bear with me a little, to cut me a little slack, even to sympathize a little with the difficulties I shall undoubtedly have in trying to figure out how much to explain, and how and when, without interrupting the narrative too much . . . because it really is quite an interesting story, if you care to think about it, which has implications for us all.

So, it was the first Saturday in March and I was going dancing at the Palais. Nothing problematic about that, obviously, given that everybody understands dancing. Even zombies dance, after a fashion. Except that it is a problem, because only skellies understand what dancing means to a skelly. To a skelly, you see, the lumpen capering that squishy folk call dancing doesn't really count as *dancing* at all, any more than what ghosts like to call "the light fantastic" seems to us to be anything more than bobbing around like a soap bubble on a breeze. Obviously, they see it differently, and obviously, we shouldn't judge, but let's just admit it, shall we? We all do.

Some folk say that it adds to afterlife's rich pattern to have all the different kinds of Postmortals lumped together in the same Ghetto, along with the lycanthropes, but let's not try to gloss over the fact that it has its downside too. Looking ahead to the various phases of the story I have to tell, that downside is going to figure quite a bit, so it would be absurd to try to ignore it. So, occasionally, there will have to be lapses in diplomacy, and this is one. Squishy folk and ghosts can't dance. They think they can, and think they do, but they can't, really—and because of that, they don't understand how much dancing means to skellies, and how important Saturday nights at the Palais—or the Guignol, or wherever—are, even to skellies who don't have young bones and aren't hoping . . . well, as I said, it was the first Saturday in spring, at least by my reckoning.

I was smitten. I was expecting, or at least hoping, to meet a certain young lady. It wasn't a date exactly, but mention had been made that we might see one another at the Palais that night, not on a one-to-one basis—Melissa always went to the Palais with her friend Salome—but on the basis that we would look forward to hanging out, and maybe pay a little more attention to one another than to the others with whom the occasion brought us into proximity.

I wasn't in love yet, exactly, but I was in the sort of mood where I might be ready to fall, if Almighty Chance gave things a nudge in the right direction. So, heading for the Palais on that particular night was an even bigger deal than usual, and . . .

But perhaps I ought to pause there, just in case I do have any naïve Larval readers, who might, at this point, be a trifle puzzled by the notion that skellies can fall in love, and what they could possibly do about it if they did. In order to offer a full explanation, obviously, I'd not only have to go into detail about virtual anatomy and physiology, but also the mysteries of virtual emotion, so to save time, I'll just say that we have all the necessary virtual equipment. I'm sorry if it seems like a disgusting thought to some people, but there it is: skellies have sex. Ghosts, vampires and lykes can have sex and they too can fall in love. Even zombies can have sex, while they're still fresh enough and the bits are still intact and can probably even fall in love. Skellies with young bones are, on average, even more likely to have sex and fall in love than skellies with old bones. I had young bones. So had Melissa.

So . . . but no, perhaps I'm going a little too fast there, and skipping over some vital issues . . . which brings me to another problem for which I might have to ask for a little tolerance. You see, there are things that I don't understand myself, and in the course of the adventure I'm going to tell you about, I ran into quite a lot of them. In fact, until I had the adventure, I had never really had occasion to think about how many things there are that I don't understand, and I had certainly never had occasion before to make a real effort to understand them.

Did I mention yet that I'm just a piano player? Well, I am. That doesn't mean I'm stupid, believe me—as I hope

I'll be able to demonstrate in telling the story—but it does mean that there are things I don't understand, and had never really thought about until I had my little adventure, but which I was forced to begin to think about when I suddenly found myself in dire danger of a fate far worse than death, and the possibility of being separated from Melissa for months, if not forever. And now I'm trying to tell the story, I have to think about them even more, because if I want to explain things to all kinds of different potential readers, then I have to make an extra effort to understand them myself. And there are things that I simply didn't understand then, and still don't.

I don't feel particularly bad about that, though, because I know now, that even the likes of Dr. Leopold Charteris and Sthenelais the Ghost Psychiatrist don't really understand, even though they pretend. So, if the world's foremost Larval expert on osteomorphic physiology and a key member of the Ghost Faculty's Inner Circle don't really understand, what chance has a skelly piano player? Or you, reader, whoever you may be? So when I say that I'll try to explain things as I go along, what I mostly mean is that I'll try to share my lack of understanding in an amicable fashion.

And one of the things that's beyond my understanding, and perhaps anyone's understanding, is why it is that skellies—or vampires, ghosts and zombies—can have sex and fall in love, given that we can't have children. Sex, for us, has no reproductive function; it just seems to make afterlife more worthwhile. So why do we have the possibility?

Much Larval sex has no reproductive function either, of course—and lycanthropes seem to be sterile with one another if not always with non-theriomorphic Larvae, although that's a whole other kettle of fish, which I won't get into—but the fact remains that one can easily see the logic, in terms of natural selection, of why Larvae have organs of reproduction and sexual urges, which can then be diverted into other patterns of motivation. Why do vampires have squishy equipment, squishy eggs or squishy semen, without being able to produce squishy children? Why do ghosts and skellies at least have virtual equipment, even though there's no virtual end product, so to speak? Even the existence of virtual sperm and ova seems to be controversial, problematic even for the likes of Dr. Charteris, because there are no microscopes to render the minutiae of virtual flesh visible—another kettle of fish I won't be getting into.

According to Dr. Charteris—forgive me for quoting him even before he's been introduced into the story— the most popular theory is that afterlife sex, like afterlife itself, is a kind of echo. It's not obvious that afterlife itself has any logic, in the context of the natural selection of biological entities. "Ergo," says Dr. Charteris, "its logic must lie in some other metaphysical context"—but that's way beyond my intellectual level, so I won't go there. I'll just stick with the notion of an existential echo; that I can understand, or I think I do. So, in his view, the various postmortal species are echoes of the prior human condition. But he's a Larva, so he would think that, wouldn't he? He thinks that his kind are the one true human race, and in his way of thinking, there's nothing the rest of us *can* be but mere echoes. But that's absurd. Larvae are larvae; their real existential purpose is to grow up, perhaps to metamorphose, perhaps to become something better.

The real mystery, it seems to me, is that so many of them fail in that latter mission. Even ghosts are rare, vampires rarer and skellies rarer still. Otherwise, they'd never have been able to lock us all up in a Ghetto, would they?

You can go too far in the other direction, of course. I never got a chance to discuss it in real depth with Sthenelais, but I'm sure that ghosts, even the members of the Ghost Faculty who consider themselves the wisest of the wise, take it for granted that they're the true human race, the one and only goal and purpose of Uncreation. They not only think that Larvae are just larvae, Nature's way of manufacturing ghosts, but they think that the rest of us are just Her mistakes: the botched jobs, the failures.

But skellies don't think like that. We wouldn't, would we? Nor do vamps, or lykes, or even zombies . . . although I can't believe that, in their slowly rotting hearts, zombies can possibly think that they might be the true goal and purpose of Uncreation. The world might be crazy, but surely it can't be that crazy.

But I'm digressing—and not, alas, for the first or last time. To get back to the story . . .

When I'd finally buffed myself up to perfection, or as near as I could get, I set out for the Palais with a spring in my step. It wasn't a long walk, but it was all uphill. I wasn't living at the bottom of the hill, obviously—that's the Ditch, where the hovels are in which incontinent zombies patiently melt into repulsive slime before oozing through the cracks in the floorboards and disappearing to the bosom of the desert—but number 227, where I had the first-floor front apartment, wasn't by any means at the salubrious end of Winding Sheet Street. I had hopes and ambitions in abundance, but I was poor, with a stop-gap job teaching music and ballet in the local school. I was the youngest skelly on the block—in terms of post-transition youth, that is, not in terms of having young bones—except for the people in 225, which was a reception house for new arrivals, so I wasn't far from the beginning of my afterlife career. In fact, I'd only just got past the stage when most females of the species automatically struck a maternally protective attitude to me, rather than my young bones putting the possibility into their virtual minds of forming a meaningful relationship, which was another reason why the possibility that I might be able to form one with Melissa seemed uniquely important to me that Saturday.

If it had been an actual date, of course, I'd have made an arrangement to call for Melissa at home, or from work—she worked shifts in the Post Office, so she didn't have Saturdays off—but it wasn't, so I set out figuring that I'd have to find her once I got to the Palais, unless she and Salome took a slightly roundabout route to get there, which intersected mine. Obviously, I was hoping that they might, but I wasn't overly confident.

I was smiling and nodding at everyone I passed in the street—even the teen zombie brothers from number 339, who were trudging up the hill to some kind of gang meet. They didn't smile back, but I assumed that it was just a matter of maintaining their image as surly teens rather than any resentment of the fact that I was overtaking them so smoothly and elegantly, or the fact that they were pupils at the school where I worked. Odd as it might seem, zombies tend to remember more of their larval memories than other Postmortals—way more than skellies, who rarely remember any personal details beyond the names their larvae had—so they actually retain family relationships, especially in instances when family members die together in some kind of accident. Obviously, a few members of all postmortal species begin their afterlives as "adolescents"—Larvae seem to become capable of transition at thirteen or so, and theriomorphs begin to show symptoms at the same age—so the school where I taught had a mixed population, but siblings were rare, except among zombies.

Most of the lykes whose paths I crossed, by contrast, responded in kind to my smile, even though they probably didn't know for sure that I was smiling. It's difficult for folk with squishy eyes to read skelly expressions, even if, like lykes, they have a certain degree of virtual sight as well as vulgar sight. It works the other way round too, of course—it's much easier for me to read the expressions of other skellies than squishy expressions, although I confess that I find it even harder to read the purely virtual expressions of ghosts, but I can tell when lykes and vamps are smiling, when the occasions arise. Lykes are generally friendly enough—except when the moon's full, obviously—and the reputation that vamps have for never cracking a smile is exaggerated. The other bony folk, I met, of course, were all smiles, virtually as well as merely toothily. Skellies are a happy crowd, in general, and on the first Saturday in spring, heading for the Palais de Danse Macabre, there wasn't a surly face to be seen.

I was on the lookout for Melissa and Salome, obviously—but they knew that, and that was presumably why they decided to sneak up behind me, having obviously decided that it was worth taking the slightly longer way around.

They came up to either side of me—they must have been practically running, although I hadn't heard them rattle—and they each took one of my arms in order to slow me down.

"Not so fast, Peterkin," said Salome—always the more mischievous of the two, "or we'll think you're trying to run away from us, and that would hurt our feelings, wouldn't it, Melissa?"

"Definitely," said Melissa.

I slowed down, drastically, nothing being further from my thoughts, rejoicing in the fact that I was actually making bodily contact with Melissa—although I have to admit that contact with Salome, whose bones were equally young and perhaps, to an unbiased virtual eye, even more elegant, was also far from unpleasant.

"I didn't even know you were there," I protested—a terrible line, given all the flirtatious things I could have said if I'd only thought of them at the time, but this is a true story, so I'm not going to lie in the attempt to make myself look wittier in retrospect than I was, or am.

"How's life down by the railway?" Salome said, as she and Melissa adjusted their own pace to fall into step with my abrupt deceleration. "Couldn't stand it myself—all that jarring when the trains go by." The railway cut across Winding Sheet Street thirty yards or so below number 227, symbolically isolating zombietown on the wrong side of the tracks, although there was quite a substantial zombie population on the upper side.

"It's not so bad," I assured her. "It's not as if there are any expresses passing through, and it's always nice to hear the bottles on the milk train rattle in the morning. Music to my ears."

"You're not bathing in *milk*, are you, Peterkin?" Salome said. "You must be hard up. Is the pay *that* bad at the ballet school?" The school was just a school, obviously, but because I taught music and ballet, Salome always referred to it as "the ballet school" when talking to me. It was a joke, of sorts.

"Of course not," I said, semi-honestly.

"Well, if you can play the piano for a bunch of galumphing squishy kids," Salome said, "I don't see why you can't play somewhere nice. You ought to work at the Palais."

"Don't be unkind, Sal," Melissa put in. "You know it's not that easy. Peterkin's young, as well as having young bones."

"There you are, Peterkin," said Salome. "You've got a defender. It must be love."

Virtual flesh can't blush, because virtual blood is invisible, but skellies can certainly look embarrassed, and Melissa did—unsurprisingly, as that was obviously Salome's intention.

"Ignore her," Melissa said. "She always gets high-spirited on Saturday evening." Which, if you think about it, is far from the most flirtatious line she could have come up with—but I forgave her for that instantly, and even decided to assume that if she'd had longer to think about it, she might have taken pleasure in finding a better one.

"There's a lot of competition in the dance halls," I told them both. "I'm getting better all the time, but I'm still learning. The fingering isn't easy when your phalanges are as stubby as mine. The top-flight skelly pianists have been at it for thirty or forty years."

"Don't worry," Salome said. "Arthritis will slow them down eventually, and make room for up-and-coming talent."

Technically, the troubles that afflict older skelly bones aren't really arthritis, but osteomorphic pathology borrows lots of terms from Larval terminology, more in a spirit of convenience than pedantry.

"I don't want to get a job just because the guy who has it is getting stiff," I said. "I want to get one on merit. Eventually, I will. It's just a matter of practicing, and waiting for a break. In the meantime, the job at the school pays the rent. It can be painful watching the squishy kids galumphing, as you put it, but some of the young skellies are very good indeed—a pleasure to teach."

"There can't be many of them, though," Melissa put in. "We're the smallest minority in the Reservation." She was making an effort to be genteel. Mostly, Ghetto-dwellers never call the Ghetto the "Reservation," although Larvae always do, if you can trust what we see of the Outside world on TV.

"Actually," I said, "the proportions of the school population aren't the same as the proportions of the adult population. Vamps are the smallest minority there, and lykes an even bigger majority in school. It must have something to do with the probability of Larvae that die young making different kinds of transition—or, in the case of lykes, metamorphosing before dying. The older teachers tell me that the proportions change over time as well, and that . . ."

"Oh, stop it," said Salome. "That's not a suitable topic for Saturday night conversation—and anyway, we're

here. It's time to stop talking altogether, and dance."
We'd only joined the queue, so we weren't inside yet, but
it was moving with efficient rapidity.

"But there'll be time for talking later," Melissa was
quick to put in, "when things slow down."

"Don't wish the evening away," Salome advised her.
"Make the most of it."

"I intend to," Melissa countered. "I always do. You'll
dance with us in the line, won't you, Peterkin?"

That was music to my ears, even though she'd said
"us." I figured that she really meant "me." I liked Salome,
of course, and was always glad to be with her in a line,
or a smaller group, but even in the line, I always thought
of it as dancing *with Melissa*, if I could contrive to be
next to her, or even just nearby. The suggestion that she
felt the same, and that she actually wanted to dance *with
me*, even in the general hurly-burly, set the space inside
my skull fizzing with a delicious dizziness that folk with
squishy brains presumably never experience—or ghosts
either, given that they don't have the echo chamber.

You need bones, even if your flesh is mostly virtual.
You really do need bones, whatever ghosts might say or
think. Trust me on that.

"Of course I will," I assured Melissa, trying to sound
as if I were doing her a favor, although I'm not sure why.
Pride, I guess. In fact, I felt anxious as well as pleased. I
felt that I'd have to deserve the privilege, that I'd have to
make a real effort. Real dancing has an extremely subtle
artistry as well as a very particular decorum—if it didn't,
it wouldn't be dancing at all, just jigging about to the
music. We bony folk take our dancing extremely seri-

ously; it's our most important sources of delight, and when a bony chap with young bones is asked to dance with two bony beauties, even in the hurly-burly of the line, it implies that a lot is expected of him.

In truth, my dancing wasn't that much more accomplished than my piano-playing, as yet, but I was working on it. I had hopes for that too. I had all kinds of hopes, in fact—which was why the last thing I needed, on that night of all nights, was to run into trouble and nearly get myself killed for a second and last time.

2

The lighting at the Palais de Danse Macabre is subdued—much less bright than the lighting at a vamp
ball or a lyke hop, but not as dark as a ghostly bob-and-
float session. Ghosts don't exclude other Postmortals
from their fun and games, any more than the rest of us
do, because we all operate on the principle that we're
all in the Ghetto together and we have to get along,
but they don't make concessions to the fact that even
hybrids who have both vulgar sight and virtual sight
find dancing in the dark a trifle challenging. We do
make allowances. The management at the Palais like to
make the environment comfortable for all comers, so
that's one of the reasons why the lighting is tastefully
subdued, but not the only one.

Actually, if I might digress for a moment again, that's
one of the other things I don't understand, and which
perhaps nobody does, whatever the Faculty and Larval
physicists might claim. Light is mysterious. You might
think that, just as there are two kinds of flesh, there are
two kinds of light, and that squishy eyes see by means of
vulgar photons, whereas virtual eyes see by means of the
virtual equivalent, but it really isn't that simple, presumably because the distinction between the two kinds of
flesh is neither as simple, nor as absolute, as it might
seem at first glance.

Obviously, given that vulgar flesh is capable of meta-morphosis into virtual flesh, there must be a sense in which, at some fundamental level, they're really the same thing, even though they seem so different, and, in the same way, vulgar light and virtual light must, at some level, be different aspects of the same phenomenon. Thus, although bone doesn't have any obvious "retinal capacity"—as Dr. Charteris would probably put it—it does have a sensitivity to vulgar light. One side-effect of that is that skellies, unlike ghosts, actually like daylight, and electric light, even though their virtual sight doesn't have the same dependency on it as squishy eyes. On the other hand, we're perfectly comfortable in dim light, in which we can see a little better than lykes or vamps, and much better than Larvae. On the other hand, we're perhaps a little less comfortable than they are in bright light.

I mention all that now, rather than saving it until certain points in the story to which it will become more relevant, because it helps to explain the scene that confronts you in the Palais on a Saturday night, when it's full to capacity. The crowd is always mostly skellies, naturally, but there are always a good number of lykes, some of whom like to pretend that they can dance and actually join the lines, although most of them just like to watch, like the vamps who come along, almost all of whom treat it as a spectator event, at least until things slow down. And there are always a few ghosts too—not Faculty members, usually, but what passes among the ghosts for ordinary folk—who probably think that they're joining in by bobbing around, and maybe even adding to the spectacle by adding an airborne component, but who are really just doing their own thing in parallel. Zombies are always thin on the ground, and if they try to jig around—as they usually do—they tend to do it in parallel too, albeit at a much lower level, in every sense of the term.

And it all happens in lighting that is not merely subdued, but also variegated, with areas of color and areas of shadow, the patterns of which make a significant contribution to the pattern and the esthetics of the dances, in ways that even skellies who aren't connoisseurs understand reasonably well, although even other Postmortals who think they are connoisseurs—and a few lykes certainly have that delusion—really don't. Because of that, the all-species-welcome policy does lead to a certain amount of confusion and awkwardness.

Do we care? I'd be lying if I simply said no, but in all sincerity, not that much. Some of us even feel that the presence of the comprehension-challenged adds a certain piquancy to the occasion, and to be perfectly honest, even if the crowd was all skelly, it certainly wouldn't be devoid of incomprehension. It takes a long time to become a connoisseur of dancing, and some people just don't have the feel for it.

I do—or, at least, I'd certainly like to think that I do. Young as I am, in more ways than one, I like to think that I have rhythm in my bones. So, I think—or was certainly eager to convince myself—had Melissa, whose bones were even younger than mine, although she'd been in the Ghetto for a while longer. That was one of the reasons, I believed then, and still believe, that she and I had a particular affinity for one another, whereas Salome, who was, purely in terms of virtual vision, the prettier of the two, didn't seem nearly as attractive to me.

So, when we got inside the hall and immediately joined a line, with me in the middle, Melissa holding my left hand and Salome my right, I immediately began to pay attention to the pattern of the lighting, and how the manner and height of the colors and the shadows ought to affect the sinuosities of the line and the steps required on the individuals therein. But I wasn't concentrating. If anything, I was trying to put thought out of my mind and let feeling take over: the feelings of the dance, primarily, although those were inevitably mingled with, and enhanced by, feelings of another sort.

Even so, in spite of that particular state of consciousness, which wasn't really susceptible of taking note of anything, I can remember very clearly noticing that among the ghosts hovering over the snaky, whirling skelly lines, there was one who wasn't bobbing, but who was just watching . . . and even though I thought at the time that it was absurd to think so, I got the impression that she was watching me. Naturally, I looked back, quite sharply, and she immediately looked away, but in a rather ostentatious fashion that suggested to me that she was doing it deliberately, precisely in an attempt to make it obvious that she hadn't been staring at me. I looked at her hard, trying to determine whether I'd seen her before, but I didn't think I had, and I'm usually quite good at remembering faces, even ghost faces. I sneaked a couple of swift glances during the next five minutes, just to see whether she was looking at me again, but she still seemed to be looking away, so I forgot about it, figuring that I didn't care anyway.

Looking back with the aid of hindsight, I know that I have to beware of "remembering" more than I could possibly have realized at the time, but I don't think I'm just imagining the fact that, even while my enraptured virtual heart was racing with the tempo of the dance, and surging at the contact of Melissa's hand, and swirling in the pattern of the steps, I thought: "What on earth is a Faculty member doing here? And why is she looking at me?"

Why did I think that, if in fact I really did? I don't know. How did I even think that I would recognize a Faculty member as a Faculty member if I saw one? I don't know that either. But I really do believe that I thought it. Perhaps it was a premonition.

The Ghost Faculty is, or at least considers itself to be, the intellectual crème-de-la-crème of Postmortality. All ghosts consider themselves to be a cut above other Postmortals, but the members of the Faculty consider themselves to be the only true philosophers among us, the only true scientists, the only true intellectuals, and only one step removed, if that, from the status of demigods. So, at least, it was said. I hadn't actually rubbed humeri at that point in my life with any member of the Faculty, and everything I "knew" about them was based, I suppose, on mere gossip.

The Ghost Faculty, it was said, had far more contact with the Outside than common folk, because they were in contact with the philosophers and scientists of the Larval community—although, of course, they considered themselves to be a cut above them too. Some members of the Faculty went Outside legally, by virtue of a special dispensation from the terms of the Treaty. The rest of us, of course, don't have any choice, because the walls of the Ghetto imprison us, but ghosts, being entirely virtual, can pass through vulgar matter, so the confinement of ghosts in the Ghetto is voluntary. Even so, they're considered to be prisoners in a legal sense, except for certain members of the Faculty, under conditions set by the Larvae powers-that-be.

Do the ghosts really observe those restrictions? How should I know? But that's the way it's supposed to be.

Because they're invisible in vulgar terms, of course, and because it's rare for Larvae to have much in the way of virtual sight, it would be almost impossible for the Larvae to know for sure whether the ghosts were holding to the Treaty or not, even though they apparently claim to have ghost-detection machinery, and even so-called ghost-traps, but in fact, so far as I know and as common rumor has always had it, ghosts are very scrupulous about keeping their promises. And most of them say, if asked, that they wouldn't want to go Outside anyway, having no reason to do so, traditional allegations regarding their penchant for haunting being mostly the product of the larval imagination.

The members of the Faculty, of course, did have a reason for going Outside, in order to participate in the Global Scientific Community, and that's why they were allowed to do so, albeit not that often. So it was said. It was also said that they didn't often show themselves in ordinary Ghetto society very frequently, and certainly not in places like the Palais de Danse Macabre on a Saturday night.

So, my question was a fair one, if I actually did pose it to myself: what was a Faculty member doing in the Palais that night, seemingly looking at me? I now know, of course, that it was Sthenelais, and that she really was watching me—but I certainly had no reason to suspect that at the time, so the truly remarkable thing is not that she was doing it, but that I somehow noticed her doing it, and actually guessed who she was and what she was doing. She, of course, would probably pour scorn on the notion that it even happened, let alone that it was a premonition, but I'm not so sure. There are lots of things I don't understand, but there also seem to be things for which I have a natural feel, of which music is only one.

Anyway, I'm recording the fact—or the apparent fact—for what it's worth. But if I really did think it, I didn't think any more about it thereafter, as I absorbed myself in the dance, the lighting, and the feel of Melissa's lovely bones in contact with mind, supplemented by the feel of the virtual flesh overlaying Melissa's lovely bones, in contact with my own virtual flesh, in which pedants call "dual quiddity."

At the time, though, the last thing I wanted to be was pedantic. And it would falsify the impression I'm trying to communicate if I started talking now about the pattern of the steps or the esthetics of line-dancing, or the psychological resonances of the spectra of virtual and vulgar light—which would be way too deep for me anyway—so I won't. Suffice it to say that I danced more enthusiastically and more extravagantly than I'd ever danced before, and I think Melissa did too. Maybe Salome did as well, but if so, I didn't notice. What I noticed was the captivation of the music, and the whiteness of the bones swirling and winding round the floor . . . especially Melissa's bones, which seemed to me to have a particular gleam that was almost a glow. You can call me shallow if you want, or delusional, but that's the way I felt. It was magic.

From an objective point of view, I suppose, at the beginning of the evening, I was only dancing with Salome and Melissa because they were on either side of me in the line, and all three of us were hurling ourselves body and soul into the traditional form of the classic *danse macabre*: follow-my-leader, as the irreverent sometimes put it. After a while, though, in any skelly farandole or carmagnole, the tempo begins to slow down somewhat, and the lines to break up, albeit in accordance with a pattern and a protocol; that's when the show-off groups began to display their virtuosity, and most of the dancers become chorus-line backers.

Because of the way our line fragmented, I was separated from Salome, and then from Melissa too, in spite of my best efforts, caught up in other quasi-compulsory formations, but I always had skill enough to maneuver my way back to them, even while the gavottes were in full swing, without having to wait for the pauses—but it was only during the pauses that fragments of conversation became possible.

"What do you think of the orchestra, Peterkin?" Salome asked me, after one slightly exhausting reel.

"It's doing its job," I opined, a trifle meanly.

"The fiddler's fingering is a bit suspect," she observed, ever the critic, "and the bongo player loses the rhythm in the crescendos."

"The pianist's smooth, though," I observed, reluctantly aware that he was a lot more fluent than me, "and the flautist's a real virtuoso."

"A touch shrill for my taste."

"They're not playing a concert," Melissa put in. "As Peterkin says, they're doing their job. It's just accompaniment. We're having fun, aren't we?"

"Oh yes," Salome agreed, "we're having lots of fun. That's what Saturday night's all about, isn't it, Peterkin?"

"Absolutely," I agreed—although I wasn't entirely sure that she wasn't being ironic—or, if she was, why. With Salome, it was sometimes difficult to tell.

We were having lots of fun, though. At least, I was, even though I became painfully aware that I still had limitations of artistic execution in spite of my feeling for the music, especially when the evening progressed to the more complicated and exotic moves. I wasn't exactly in demand for the showier maneuvers, although Salome and Melissa weren't the only ladies prepared to try a little trip and glide with me, and they weren't so much in demand themselves that the real dandies were keen to whisk them away—about which Salome, at least, seemed a trifle resentful—but I certainly didn't disgrace myself, in spite of my slight self-dissatisfaction, and I was secretly quite glad that Melissa wasn't being urgently pressured by the ace metatarsal-shufflers.

By the time exhaustion began to set in, we had almost settled into being a couple, especially as Salome had collected an insistent admirer of her own in a fellow named Phil, whom I only knew by sight, although I had formed the impression somehow that he fancied himself as a bit of an intellectual. I didn't think he had much chance with Salome, when I first saw them gravitating together, but she seemed to be tolerating his attentions well enough, and her deflection allowed me to focus even more closely on Melissa than I'd ever had a chance to do on previous evenings at the Palais, or when we occasionally ran into one another during the week, at the Post Office or elsewhere.

When we decided to sit one out, we sat down on one of the banquettes against the wall, and I turned toward her in a seriously interested fashion, resting my left hand on the wall, not because I needed the support but because I hoped it made for an engaging pose.

"Have you met the new folk who've moved in next door to you yet?" she asked me.

"I introduced myself, said hello and told them to ask if they needed anything," I told her, "but you know what new arrivals are like—still somewhat disorientated. Once they get their bearings, though, they'll probably move on. People don't tend to stay long in 225, precisely because it's a place where new people get lodged. 227 might be architecturally identical, but culturally, the two facets of the terrace are worlds apart." I cursed myself silently for sounding so much like a schoolteacher.

"There don't seem to be so many new arrivals these days," she observed, "or is that just my impression?"

"No, I think you're right," I assured her, although I really had no idea. "Not such a bad thing, given that the Ghetto's a trifle crowded, and the chances of getting the Larvae to pull back the walls and give us more space are probably slim to none."

"They're definitely building another Reservation, though. I saw it on the TV news yesterday."

"I didn't know," I said, defensively. "I don't watch TV that much—too busy practicing, trying to get my playing up to scratch."

"It was on the City channel, even though it's Outside business. It concerns us, obviously."

To tell the truth, I didn't pay much attention to the City channel either back then, given that it was mostly run by lykes and for lykes. Skellies hardly got a look in, except for specialist programming, in proportion to the size of our minority. These days, I take more interest.

"I suppose it does," I said, although I didn't really think that it concerned me all that much. "I don't want to emigrate myself, but there are plenty of folk who would, even though they'd only be swapping one Ghetto for another. Where are they building it?"

"Australia. And there's already talk of starting a third, in Africa."

"They won't get that many volunteers for transplantation, then. Isolated as we are, I suppose there's a sense in which it doesn't really matter whether we're in America or on the Moon, but the heat's bad enough here, without our being transplanted to the Outback or the Sahara—which are, I presume, the sites they've selected."

"Talking politics?" said Salome flopping down into the chair beside me. "That's not like you, Peterkin."

Phil remained standing, looking down at the three of us.

"Not really," I said, defensively. "Just light chat. It's Saturday night, after all, and the first week of spring."

"Time for dancing," Phil put in. "Couldn't agree more—as long as we keep an ear alert for distant thunder."

"What do you mean?" Melissa asked.

"Just because it's spring, it doesn't mean that everything in the garden is rosy," Phil observed, in the dry fashion that people who fancy themselves to be intellectuals always adopt when being condescending. "But Peterkin's right—it's Saturday night, time for living life . . . which is to say, afterliving afterlife. Isn't it a drag to be stuck with a language devised by Larvae for describing the larval condition? We don't eat and we don't drink, but we can at least be merry, for tomorrow . . . is Sunday. Then Monday, and back to work. How's life at ballet school, Peterkin?" He'd obviously picked up the phrase from Salome.

"Can't complain," I said, although I could have—not least at the slight curl of his lip when he pronounced the word *ballet*. "How's life as a . . . what is it you do, exactly?"

"My official title is *correspondent*," Phil replied, not taking offense. "Limitations of Larval language again, although I'm pretty sure that they don't show much limitation in inventing less apposite terms for me. Frustrating, actually, I must confess, as the copy I deliver tends to be heavily filtered before it reaches its intended audiences. But hey, we're here to dance, not to wallow in our woes, right? Fancy a twirl, Melissa?"

And with that, he whisked Melissa away, without even waiting for her to signal her consent, leaving me and Salome together.

I didn't suppose for a moment, that she was any less chagrined than I was, but there was no way in the world she would have let on. "Don't look so disappointed," she said. "You'll damage my ego."

"I'm not disappointed," I lied. "How could anyone be disappointed at suddenly finding himself alone with the most beautiful girl at the ball?"

It wasn't actually untrue, allowing for a little poetic license. If skellies had been the kind of folk to hold held beauty contests, Salome probably fit the consensus ideal as well as anyone I knew, but, partly for that reason, I

34

found Salome a trifle intimidating . . . even more intimidating, that is, than I found most girls of my postmortal age. While I was still hesitating as to whether the stylish thing to do was to try to whisk her back on to the floor the way Phil had just whisked Melissa, she took the wind out of my sails.

"You really wouldn't want to go somewhere else, if you got the chance?" she said, in a serious manner that didn't seem at all like her usual self. "I would."

"If it were really somewhere else," I conceded, "I suppose I'd have to give it some thought. But trading a Ghetto in the middle of one desert for a Ghetto in the middle of another doesn't really qualify."

"Even if it were less crowded and more . . . specialized?"

"Specialized?" I said. "You think the Larvae are considering splitting the postmortal populations up? Why would they do that? We have our differences, but as multicultural societies go, we seem to be rubbing along quite well . . . and why would the Larvae care, even if we weren't?"

"There are people who think that when the Larvae lumped us all in here together they weren't just expelling us from their world but hoping that we'd massacre one another," Salome agreed, soberly. "Judging us by themselves, I guess." I got the impression that when she said "people" she meant Phil—which implied that he'd been talking politics even while they were on the floor.

"That's not really fair," I said. "There's a certain hypocrisy in their leaders saying that they built the City as a place of safety to protect us from persecutions, but as an alternative to the genocides that they were capable by then of carrying out, it was surely the lesser of the two evils. It was better, too, than maintaining the old skeptical pretense that we didn't exist, that we were just legends and figments of diseased imagination."

She seemed mildly surprised. "So you *can* talk politics?" she said. "You obviously have hidden depths." She laughed at that, although it wasn't really a joke.

"I may be just a piano player," I said, "but I'm not stupid."

"No," she said, softening her tone. "Don't mind me. You're right, anyway—no point in thinking about such things until the possibility is actually on the table. Live in the moment, count your blessings, and all the other clichés. Just dance . . . especially on Saturday night, and face tomorrow when it comes."

"But you disapprove anyway . . . almost as much a Phil?"

"Phil doesn't disapprove—he just can't do it. Neither can I. Nor can Melissa, although she puts on an act."

"Everybody does," I said. "I can't remember the specifics of my larval existence any better than the next skelly, but I'm certain that it was no different then. Existence *is* putting on an act . . . the point is to be comfortable in the role, if you can . . . and at least to enjoy the dancing. Shall we?"

She shook her head. "I'll sit out a little longer, if you don't mind. Go and join Melissa and Phil. She'll be pleased, and he'll be obliged to pretend not to mind. And if he throws a slight fit and comes back to sit with me . . . well, who'll complain?"

Even though virtual flesh doesn't blush, it has its subtle ways of showing embarrassment, and I knew that mine had to be visible to Salome. I had to do what I was told, though, even if I did have a fearful suspicion that Phil might regard my intrusion as a challenge, and, far from returning to chat intimately with the lovely Salome, he might start showing off his best moves in order to outshine me in Melissa's eyes.

He probably thought about it, but he definitely fancied Salome that little bit more than he fancied Melissa, and it's not impossible that he had only whisked her away in order to separate her from Salome, in the hope that I would do exactly what Salome had told me to do. Personal politics can sometimes be just as tortuous as the other kind. At any rate, he let me cut in, and went meekly back to sit with Salome.

Almost as soon as he had bowed out, leaving Melissa and me twirling together, the music mellowed considerably, and it became perfectly feasible to chat as well as dance, at least in snatches, even while I was trying to show off.

"Is Salome all right?" Melissa asked me.

"I think so," I said, and had to pause before adding: "She does seem a little worried." After a further move, I added: "Has she said anything?"

"Nothing specific." After another pause, she added: "I thought she might have asked Phil . . ." I had to wait for the rhythm to oblige before she completed the sentence with: ". . . to take me away so she could talk to you."

I was surprised by that, because the idea seemed so unlikely, but also delighted, because it implied strongly that she would have been jealous if that had been the case. I didn't want to read too much into it, though, in case I was building up unrealistic hopes.

"No . . ." I told her, eventually adding, with only slight exaggeration: ". . . She could hardly wait to get rid of me."

"She likes Phil, then?" was her next contribution to the punctuated dialogue.

"Or doesn't like me," I supplied, with conscientious modesty.

Perhaps it was a trifle too conscientious, because her sarcastic comeback was: "Who could possibly not like you?"

To which my heroically false modest reply was: "Who could possibly not prefer Phil?"

That was too blatantly fishing for a compliment, alas, and she wasn't about to rise to the bait—and virtual flesh doesn't blush, so it wasn't possible to guess her reaction by means of mere appearances.

So we set all philosophical questions aside for a while, and just danced, and cultivated our intimacy silently while we danced a few fancy reels. Skellies can do that . . . or maybe it's just an effect of dancing, which even works on squishy flesh.

I'm sure, though, that I was more exhilarated than usual, and more entranced, and still feeling a little residual delight at the idea that there had been a hint of jealousy or apprehension in Melissa's suspicion that Salome might have wanted to have me to herself for a few minutes, and a hint of relief in her discovery that it wasn't so.

It's not surprising, I suppose, that my favorite dances are reels. I'm really not that fond of the waltzing, let alone the ensemble pieces where everyone on the floor has a definite part to play within some complicated scheme that only the oldsters really know by heart. Even though I have a feel for all kinds of dancing, my favorite has always been dancing *à deux*, and even then, being able to do my own thing rather than following a set progression of steps. I've got shorter than average legs as well as shorter than average fingers, and I can't glide and stride with the same elegance as taller folk, but I can twirl and reel as well as anyone.

But the evening was winding down, and I knew that it would soon be time to go home again, so regret began to set in as well.

Looking back on the evening clinically, I suppose I had danced with a lot of other people as well as Salome and Melissa, but there was no doubt in my mind that what I had been doing, for every single minute, was dancing with Salome and Melissa, and that it was dancing with Melissa that had really mattered. I hoped that she felt the same way, and it was an intoxicating hope.

I know that there are some people, not all of them Larvae or squishy Postmortals, who might think it absurd for me to talk like that, in terms of being intoxicated, given that we bony folk don't drink alcohol any more than we drink water, and because whatever virtual flesh has to replace hormones and neurons can't reproduce the effects of alcohol on squishy flesh in any literal sense. Believe me, though, it does make sense to speak of pleasant intoxication, or getting high on amorous emotion.

As to what's actually happening, in physiological terms, there's a whole slew of Mad Scientists working on such problems at the City University, and they're not all members of the Ghost Faculty, who would probably keep any discoveries they made strictly to themselves.

There are lykes, vamps and skellies, all taking a fervent interest in the issue, but they don't seem to have made a lot of progress since the Ghetto was first isolated, which is knocking on for a century now. Uncle Paulus, who's the oldest skelly in the place, is fond of saying that it's because there isn't enough madness in their method, but he's just trying to be witty.

In consequence, I can't give you any kind of technical explanation of my intoxication, even if you want one, which you probably don't. Suffice it to say that I was in a very good mood when the evening ended, albeit one edged by the regret that I'd soon have to say goodnight to Melissa, and might not see her again for days. Was I in love by then? I thought so—and is there any more to being in love than thinking you are? On the other hand, I also thought that the feeling I got while I danced with Melissa must be quite different from the feelings my larval self must have had when experiencing what squishy folk call lust. I don't know why I'm so convinced of that—how can I possibly know what squishy folk feel?—but I was. I'm certain, too, that what squishy folk call "real" is only an illusion of organic chemistry, and that virtual reality is the only virtuous kind.

Anyhow, all things considered, I had had a really good time.

3

I was feeling quite deliciously exhausted by the time I said a reluctant final goodnight to Salome and Melissa at the corner where I had to turn off into Winding Sheet Street, while they followed the contour of the hill to the misnamed Popular Gardens. I was glad to see that Melissa seemed more than a trifle reluctant too, but neither she nor Salome said anything to me about making a firm date to meet up again, even the following weekend. Perhaps I should have—in fact I'm sure I should—but somehow, my virtual tongue couldn't spit the audible words out.

I got the impression that Melissa, at least, wished that I wasn't quite as shy as I suddenly was, although Salome didn't seem to care. She was still a trifle out of sorts, but that might have been because Phil hadn't had any occasion to walk that far with us, as he lived in the opposite direction, practically on the outskirts of Vampville, near the Communication Station.

It was pretty late by the time we went our separate ways, but the ball up at the Gothic Castle was still in full swing—the drinking, if not the dancing—and lycanthropes tend to call it a night early, when there isn't a full moon, even on Saturdays. Ghostly congregations tend to be quiet as well as dark, so it's difficult to tell what they're up to and when, although I strongly suspect that they love being mysterious, and are probably much more active when there are no skellies around and the danger of their being seen is much reduced.

In consequence of the relative scarcity of other folk, there was hardly anyone around in the streets to smile at once the crowd from the Palais had thinned out and I'd turned into Winding Sheet Street. Unfortunately, the hardly anyone included an entire zombie gang, who were loitering—although probably without any specific intent—just uphill from the front gate of 227.

The whole gang seemed to be in a fractious mood. It seemed to me that they hadn't had as much fun as they thought they were somehow entitled to have on a Saturday night—or, indeed, any fun at all. They seemed resentful of my obvious good mood as soon as they caught sight of me and watched me coming down the hill. Nine times out of ten they would probably just have shuffled aside to let me through, with a few muttered insults, but the teens from number 339 were either unusually bored or wanted to put on a show of bravado for their mates. The two brothers hesitated for a moment or two, but temptation carried them away and they deliberately blocked my way.

"Had a good time, Skelly?" the older of the two said, slobbering as he sneered, in the way that only zombies can.

"Fair to middling," I said, cautiously, not knowing whether it would annoy them more if I showed too much enthusiasm or none at all.

"Hot night at the Palais?" his younger brother put in. "Lots of shaking and rattling?"

"Everybody has their thing," I said, mildly. "I shake and rattle. How about you boys? Had a good evening?"

"Same as always," the younger brother replied. As a relatively new Postmortal, who could probably remember enough of larval life to think that he hadn't had nearly enough of it, he was still in relatively good condition, and he enunciated his words more clearly than the average zombie. "You know how it is—people looking down on us, calling us names, shooing us away. *You* know— *everybody* looks down on zombies, but you bonebags are the worst."

"That's not true," I assured him. "We live in the same neighborhood, don't we? We're good neighbors"

It probably wasn't the best argumentative point to make at that particular moment. The reason that poorer bony folk live in the same neighborhoods as zombies is partly that, like zombies, they don't have any reason to live in mortal fear of flesh-eaters who might forget their manners, but mostly because they don't have any choice. If they did, they'd avoid zombies just as much as everybody else does. It certainly isn't because we have any particular affection for zombies, and zombies are well aware of that.

"You think *everything* with flesh is unspeakably vulgar, don't you?" the kid went on, some pent-up resentment evidently coming belatedly to the boil. Zombies don't usually use phrases like "unspeakably vulgar," but the kid was fresh; his own brain hadn't yet had time to rot into stinking porridge, and the supplies that come in on the brain-train nowadays are mostly lab-grown from tissue-cultures, so he hadn't confused himself with too many chewed-up relics of larval memories, the way older zombies tended to do back in the day. His friends were mostly in worse condition, but that only encouraged them to mutter in support, admiring his cleverness and egging him on.

"We're all Postmortal, mate," I said, soothingly. "We're all in the same Ghetto. The people who *invented* scorn are the Outsiders. We don't need it here, do we?"

"Are you trying to mess with us?" the older brother said.

"Are you *laughin'* at us?" put in one of the other members of the gang.

The answer was *no* in both cases, but they obviously weren't asking me because they wanted to know. "I can't help the silly grin," I said, trying to sound regretful. "I don't have anything to cover it up with."

"'E's takin' the piss," said another member of the gang, clearly an import from England. "Thinks 'e's *so* much cleverer than we are, *so* much better, because he don't 'ave to eat or breathe—just soak 'imself in whitewash."

"Fleshless creep," another chipped in. "You ain't any better than us."

"There's no point in this, lads," I said, trying to sound more world-weary than nervous. "As you can clearly see, I'm not carrying anything you can eat or steal. Let's just call it a night, shall we?"

"Calling us thieves now, are you?" said the younger of the brothers from number 339. "Saying that we'd eat the flesh off our neighbors' backs?"

"Well," I said, my self-control snapping, "you *would* eat the brains out of your neighbors' skulls, if the brain-train didn't keep you adequately provisioned, wouldn't you? Just as the vamps would be after the lykes' blood if *their* supply trains stopped running? We can't help what we are. That's afterlife . . . except for the lykes, who aren't Postmortals at all, but just mortals who got a raw deal from Almighty Chance."

That was a mistake. Nobody likes being lectured, and zombies really don't like it, because they hate their own stupidity and don't like it when anyone gives the impression of trying to make them feel it. Really, I should have known better. I did, in fact, but sometimes we skellies get rattled. That's one of those many true words typically spoken in jest.

The ex-English lout mumbled once again that I was "taking the piss"—older zombies have a tendency to repetition—and several others backed him up with insults that only lost a little of their venom in their utter incoherence.

"Grab him!" said one of the strangers. "Teach him a lesson!"

I think the younger brother hesitated then, probably realizing that things were getting out of hand, and remembering that he was my neighbor, even if his friend wasn't. But he capitulated to peer pressure, and stifled any objection that he might have had.

Even skellies with shorter than average legs are agile enough to dodge zombies in any normal circumstance, and outdistance them in three strides, but they were all around me, and there was no viable gap through which I could slip. Having decided to grab me, they did so easily enough, and had no difficulty holding on to me, no matter how hard I struggled.

Figuring out how to teach me a lesson was something else, though. If only the one who had suggested that they grab me hadn't been so hyped up, or if the younger brother had been willing to put a word in to moderate their sudden enthusiasm, they'd probably just have roughed me up a bit and let me go, but one of the gang suddenly had a surge of evil inspiration—or what passes for a surge of inspiration, if you're a zombie.

"Let's tie him to the railway track," the inspired one said.

Again, the younger brother looked as if he were about to object, but again, he stifled the objection.

"Come *on*!" I said, impatiently. "We're neighbors, damn it! Show a bit of common sense."

It was entirely the wrong thing to say, of course. You should never accuse a zombie of a lack of common sense—even zombies can be hurt by manifest truth. They dragged me down the hill: not all the way to the lower depths of Winding Sheet Street, but only to the cutting through which the railway ran. I tried as hard as I could to pull away, but there were too many of them, and their fists, once clenched, exerted a grip that was far too solid.

Ordinarily, I'd still have been all right. Nine times out of ten, they wouldn't have been able to find anything handy to bind me to the track with, and ninety-nine times out of a hundred they'd have botched any knots they tried to tie in whatever they did find—but some imbecile railway employee had been mending the wire fence beside the track, and he'd left an entire bale of the stuff just lying around when he'd knocked off for the weekend.

The zombies didn't have to tie any kind of a knot that would have been a test of dexterity—all they had to do was thread the wire underneath the track between two sleepers, and then wind it round and round my wrist repeatedly. Even that might have been okay if they hadn't had a means of cutting the wire, but one of them had a blade. He was too stupid to care about taking the edge off it by sawing through the wire, so he did, enabling them to could repeat the procedure with the second track and my other wrist.

Then they ran away, laughing and gurgling simultaneously, the way only zombies can. Even the two brothers didn't look back, let alone think of coming back to help me get free, as good neighborliness would surely have commanded even zombies to do if they hadn't thought it was hilarious.

What I'd said to Salome and Melissa about not being bothered by the jarring as the trains went past wasn't entirely true. I'd got used to it, but not before I'd become acutely aware of the pattern of the timetable. I knew full well, therefore, there were only two trains scheduled to run between midnight Saturday and Sunday daylight, one of which was the milk train, which wouldn't be going through for at least five hours. The other, unfortunately, was the last cross-town passenger service, which made an extra circular trip in the early hours of Sunday morning to carry the drunk and the exhausted back home from the ball at the Gothic Castle. I knew that it was due in less than fifteen minutes, and that it was very rarely late.

At first, stupidly, I tried to pull myself free by means of simple brute force, but that only tightened the wires around my wrists. Then I tried to curl my fingers around in the hope of getting a grip on the trailing end of one or other of the tangles. Some skellies, I suppose, would have had fingers long enough to do that. I didn't.

By the time I realized that I'd have to try and work the wire loose with my toes, I'd wasted nearly half the available time—and by the time I'd managed to get my right foot into a position in which the unpracticed toes could get clumsily to work, I'd used up half the remainder.

We bony folk can, of course, recover from the occasional break or separation—even from multiple breaks and separations, with the aid of a clever osteopath and lots of bed-rest—but reassembly requires certain conditions to be met. First of all, you have to be able to find all the bits. Secondly, and more importantly, the bits have to escape serious crushing, mangling or other permanent distortion. Thirdly, and most importantly of all, the virtual matter that holds creatures like us together, and gives us the ability to dance even though we no longer have any muscles, not only has to be preserved but maintained in its integrity.

Postmortals are still mortal. For us, dying isn't something that you only have to do once. Nobody remembers the first time, at least in any detail, but nobody dares to think that it wasn't extremely unpleasant, or that it might seem any less horrible the second time around just because we've done it before.

Even if all three of the essential criteria for osteal reassembly are met, the cartilaginous sinews that hold the bones together rarely retain their full elasticity, or the bones their full strength, once they've been seriously injured. Reassembly can seriously damage your dancing ability—and, even more importantly, in my case, your ability to play the piano. I hadn't even reached my fully

48

potential yet in that regard; any ambition I had to be something more than a rehearsal pianist at the local school was highly unlikely to survive a close encounter with a train, even if the impact didn't wipe me out completely.

I made what haste I could with the aid of my toes, but I was still loosening the wire when I heard the train whistle as it came toward the slight bend at the gasworks.

That was when the terror really struck deep into my virtual soul.

I was still working at it when I saw the engine's headlights in the distance.

The terror was still increasing, although I didn't understand how it still had any margin for growth.

I was *still* working at it when I smelled the oily heat of the thing bearing down upon me, at what seemed to be a far faster speed than the forty miles an hour it must actually have been doing.

That was when the terror reached a pitch that I would have thought incredible had I still been capable of thinking at all.

In fact, I was working at it until the very last second, when I finally managed to wrest my right hand free and hurl myself away to the left of the track, dragging my captive left hand down into the gap on the outer side of the rail, whose cross-section was shaped like a thick H lying on its side.

Luckily, the wheels—which were safely confined to the inside of the track—sliced through the wire as if it were butter. The consequent crushing sensation was excruciating, but nothing actually tore or broke, and the bones in my wrist weren't irreparably damaged.

By the time the last of the carriages had passed by—which seemed to take a long time, in spite of the speed at which the engine had been moving—I'd been able to roll away.

I got to my feet, nursing my injured wrist. I knew that what had just happened to me qualified as attempted murder, in legal terms, but I also knew that the zombie gang-members were too stupid to have thought of it in those terms. Even if the City police hadn't been lycanthropes almost to a man, and therefore very sensitive to pleas of diminished responsibility, zombies really were far less accountable for actions of that sort than folk who were fully capable of rational thought and moral responsibility. Making a complaint would simply have stirred up trouble, for me as well as for the gang members. No good could come of it.

I had had a narrow escape, but I had escaped. I was bruised, but not seriously damaged.

Or so I thought, at the time.

Perhaps you might reckon me foolish. Perhaps you might deem me cowardly. But I decided simply to let it go and not to make a fuss. And looking back, knowing what I know now, I certainly don't think that I made the wrong decision.

At any rate, I dusted myself off, and I went home and had a *very* long bath.

4

My left wrist was still hurting when I got up in the morning, but not so badly that I felt that it qualified as an emergency. Even so, I didn't want to put off going to the osteopath until Monday morning, and I needed a sick note, in order to explain to the school that I wouldn't be able to play then, and perhaps for several more days. Skellies aren't fetishistic about rest days, and they don't put a great deal of pressure on doctors, even though the ones we have are distinctly thin on the ground. I rang the surgery at nine and the doctor on call kindly arranged an appointment for me at three p.m.

The osteopath, Dr. Setlow, X-rayed my wrist, palpated it very carefully, and duly confirmed that even though the hand was usable, I might need as long as a week to recover the full use of my virtual sinews.

"You can probably play the piano after a fashion even now," he told me, "but I wouldn't advise it. You should certainly give it a rest for at least three days before you go back to work."

I trusted his judgment—far more, at least, than I'd have trusted a lyke or a vamp physician, even though the ones in the City are supposed to be trained in virtual medicine as well as handing out pills.

When I explained to him what had happened, the doctor nodded sympathetically, as if it were the kind of thing that he had to deal with all the time, although I knew full well that it must have been an exceedingly rare occurrence, if not unique.

"Damn zombies," he said. "Scum of the earth. It's not just the Ghetto that'd be a much better place if all the dead who came back at all came back as bony folk. The whole world would be a better place. There probably wouldn't *be* any so-called Reservation if it weren't for that kind of ambulatory slime. Even the bigots among the Larval could surely get along with bony folk and ghosts, if bony folk and ghosts were the only kinds of Postmortals there were, and they could make *ad hoc* arrangements to cope with the kinds of problems that vamps and lykes pose, but zombies . . . well, their existence drags us all down, and prejudice against them rubs off on all Postmortals, no matter how distinct we are as species."

I wasn't entirely sure that I'd have enjoyed living on the Outside, as a member of a species outnumbered a million to one by the Larvals, any more than I liked living in the Ghetto, where my kind was only outnumbered on a scale of hundreds to one, but I didn't make that objection to the doctor.

"I'll just put a poultice on this for now," he summed up, "in order to help the bones and the connective cartilage regenerate fully. This time next week, they'll be as good as new."

"Thanks," I said. "It could have been a lot worse. I'm trying to think of it as a test of character—evidence of my competence under pressure. I certainly didn't keep a cool head, mind. You know that old skellies' tale about being scared to life?"

If the osteopath had been able to widen his grin, he probably would have. "I know it," he agreed.

"Well, that's all that I could think of at the moment when I was convinced that the locomotive was going to shatter me into a hundred pieces and scatter them along a mile of track. I'd got to such a pitch of anxiety that I wasn't worried about death. *If I get out of this*, I thought, *I'll get scared back to life, and have to go round the whole bloody merry-go-round again*. Ridiculous, or what?"

"We can't help what comes into our minds at moments of great stress," Dr. Setlow assured me. "Panic does strange things. Perhaps the idea, absurd as it is, provided that little bit of extra incentive you needed to free yourself sufficiently to get out of the path of the train."

"Perhaps," I agreed.

"In any case," he observed, as he anointed a bandage with some kind of oily liquid and began to wind it round my left wrist, "the Larval state can't be that bad, even if it is only one step removed from zombiedom in terms of the yuck factor—the people living it seem to cope with it well enough. It's said that some of them even enjoy it. Their flesh is programmed with a survival instinct, just as ours is."

"Yes," I said, flippantly, "but in them it's a mental disease. Even they know that, really. What is it that they're so fond of saying: *The best thing of all is not to be born, and after that, to die young?*"

"That do say that," the osteopath agreed, "but the ones who haven't been able to avoid being born are rarely in a hurry to become Postmortal. Can't blame them for that, when so many of them don't make it at all, and those that do are more likely, statistically speaking, to achieve zombie Postmortality than our kind, or complete virtuality—which ghosts, of course, consider to be the only proper culmination of existence. Personally, I like bones, but we would wouldn't we?"

"Bones are beautiful," I agreed, content to quote the cliché—and, I must admit, thinking more about Melissa's bones as I said it than my own. "But Mother Nature's very careless, don't you think, in achieving her ends? The rate of attrition is horrific, even if it weren't for such deviations as vampirism and zombiedom."

"Nature isn't maternal and doesn't have ends," said Dr. Setlow, sternly. "She's just an agent of Almighty Chance. We're all just accidents of mutation, subject to the winnowing of natural selection. A severe attrition rate is the cost of evolution. Ghosts have no more right to think of themselves as the pinnacle of some kind of purposeful creation than larval humans—or beetles, for that matter. You'll never get a Larva to admit that virtual brains can be as intelligent as material ones, let alone more so, and the City University doesn't look like proving them wrong any time soon, in spite of the best efforts of the Ghost Faculty." He secured the bandage with a safety-pin. "There you go—come back tomorrow morning and the nurse will change the dressing. By Wednesday, we'll probably be able to dispense with it entirely."

Having finished the poultice, he stepped back to admire his handiwork. It felt clammy and cold, but even while he was writing me a sick note, it seemed to me that it was beginning to help, at least in the sense of soothing the pain. I assumed that the liquid was steeping the virtual flesh while coating the bone and cartilage, where, at the very least, it was having an anesthetic effect. I wish I could explain to you how pain signals from material bones are transmitted through virtual flesh to a virtual brain, but I can't. I asked Dr. Charteris once, but once he started droning on about "materiovirtual synapses" and "metamorphic acetylcholine transitions" I lost him completely.

I went home and phoned the school to tell them I wouldn't be in the following day, and that I would drop a sick note in the post. The deputy head, who took the call, was noticeably less sympathetic than the osteopath when I had explained what had happened, even though she was a lyke, and had just as low an opinion of zombiekind as he had.

"That's what happens when you live in a bad neighborhood, Peterkin," she told me.

"Living in a bad neighborhood is what happens when you get paid the kind of wage you can earn playing piano in a school for vamp and theriomorph kids who think they can lean to dance," I told her, rather undiplomatically, even though I had been careful not to use the word *lyke*, or even *lycanthrope*, substituting the preferred term.

"This is the finest School of Performing Arts in the City," she told me, primly. "Our students are the crème-de-la-crème. You're a perfectly competent pianist, Peterkin, but you're not really equipped to understand ballet, and criticizing your pupils is a poor way to behave. Think yourself lucky that you'll still have a job to come back to on Monday week." As an afterthought, she added: "I hope your hand makes a full recovery," without specifying whether she hoped it for my sake, hers or the sake of the pupils.

A few minutes after I'd put the phone down, the doorbell rang. I felt a twinge of optimistic hope in thinking that it might be Melissa and Salome, having somehow heard about my accident through the bony grapevine, coming to wish me a rapid recovery.

It wasn't; the news hadn't traveled all the way to Popular Gardens as yet, but it had reached as far as next door. It took me a couple of seconds to recognize the caller as one of the newcomers from 225, and even then he had to remind me of his name.

"Jack," he said. "We met briefly on Friday evening. I'm . . ."

"One of the new tenants at 225," I filled in, so that he wouldn't think that I was completely stupid. "Come in."

He came in and sat down. "We heard what happened," he said, sounding genuinely concerned. "Those wretched zombies are actually bragging about it, as if it were a joke. We were horrified—and, I have to admit, a little scared, especially the womenfolk. We're new here, obviously, and had no idea what to expect, but this . . ."

"It's not typical," I assured him. "Probably unique in afterliving memory." I held up my wrist. "Anyway, I'm fine. The doctor says that it'll be as right as rain in a few days. I suspect the poultice is just a gesture, to make me think that he's taking action, and maybe to stimulate the placebo effect."

"I'm glad to hear it," he said. "But you could have been killed."

"That wasn't the intention," I said. "You have to remember that zombies really are stupid. To them, it really was just a joke—nasty, but still a joke. The kids from

339 weren't the instigators—they just got dragged along by peer pressure."

"That's extremely generous of you—but there are police here, aren't there? Surely you ought to have informed them."

"Nothing would have come of it, given that I got away with little more than a virtual sprain; it isn't worth the hassle."

"Perhaps we . . ." he began.

"Don't even think abut it," I told him. "The last thing we need in the neighborhood is an escalation of resentment and hostility. We all have to live together, whether we like it or not, and we have to make allowances. It was a thousand-to-one chance that they found the wire and managed to wind it tightly enough to bring me to the brink of disaster. Trust me, let it go. You'll soon get used to the way things work around here. Have you've started the retraining program? Ours, that is—anything the Larvae told you while you were still Outside awaiting deportation will have been utter bullshit, given that the members of the so-called induction team have probably never set foot in the Ghetto, let alone have any conception of what being a skelly is like."

"We've only just started," he said. "One introductory session on Friday before the weekend break. We start again at nine o'clock Monday. I can understand that everything here is just routine to you, but . . . well, you can probably remember what it was like coming back. They tell me I'm one of the luckier ones, amnesia-wise. I can actually remember my name—the first one, at least—and I don't have any language loss. It's only the personal details that have gone. When I woke up, I could even remember a lot of those, briefly, but then they faded away, like a dream."

"That's exactly what it was," I told him. "Once we've made the metamorphosis, the personal aspects of Larval existence really do become a dream, something the virtual memory isn't programmed to retain. It's only the elements of that experience which qualify as general knowledge that make the transit from the material memory to the virtual one—and as you say, a lot of metamorphosites lose part of that too. Ghosts usually lose far more, although getting them to admit it is hard. Vampires tend to hang on to much more personal stuff, as you'd expect, given that they retain so much more of their material flesh, but I'm not entirely convinced that it's a blessing."

Jack shook his head, to express his continuing sense of disorientation. "It's weird," he said, "I can't remember going to school, as a Larva, but I have knowledge in my head that I must surely have been taught at school—except that I can't help suspecting that it was distorted, especially with regard to the history and details of Postmortal existence."

"Any misconceptions you've inherited probably didn't come from school," I told him. "So far as I can gather, Larval schools take the business of teaching kids about the history and possibilities of Postmortal existence very seriously, although the fact that we've all been banished to what they call the Reservation does have a distancing effect. Most of the misconceptions, and all of the worst prejudices, come from TV, especially drama series. Apparently, there's something called the internet now, which is even worse as a vehicle of misinformation, but we don't have that in the Ghetto, because of what is euphemistically termed 'communication management'—censorship to honest folk like you and me. There's a sense in which our entire community is being held incommunicado."

"I remember what the internet is," Jack agreed. "I just can't remember actually doing anything with it. Perhaps I didn't. I'm pretty sure that I was just a builder, not a smart person."

"You might have reason to be glad about that," I said. "People who can carry habitual artisanal skills through metamorphosis are in short supply here, even among the lykes. A skelly who has any kind of inherited manual skills will find it a lot easier to get well paid employment than someone whose hands were apparently only trained during his larval phase to play the piano."

Jack's eyes went to the dressing on my wrist. "Doubly inconvenient for you, then," he observed.

"Indeed," I agreed. "It could be worse, though. As long as the wrist recovers, I'll still have a job. Given that I'm working for lykes, I could easily have been dumped. Luckily, theriomorphs don't tend to become musicians, even though they like theater, including musical theater. Nobody knows why."

"That was practically the first mantra we were taught on Friday," Jack observed, wryly. "*Nobody knows why.* Considering that it's been nearly a hundred years since the Reservation was set up, and nearer two hundred since the existence of ghosts, vampires and werewolves was officially admitted and serious scientific study of the conditions began, you'd have expected more progress. We were the last to be acknowledged, obviously, thanks to the ancient Egyptian habit of wrapping us in bituminous bandages, but even so . . . we all have the same kind of virtual flesh, allegedly. How can it still be so mysterious?"

"The fact that it's invisible and intangible doesn't help," I pointed out.

"So are atoms and electrons, but the Larvae can still make nuclear bombs and all kinds of electrical gadgets."

"They're very tiny, and rather quirky, but they belong to the same basic order of matter as squishy flesh and shovels," I pointed out. "Virtual matter is a whole other kettle of fish, which moves in mysterious ways its wonders to perform. Interspecies rivalries don't help. If the Ghost Faculty and the other staff at the University worked in closer cooperation, progress would probably be smoother, but they can't even work in reasonable association with the Vampire Faculty . . . who, in their turn, regard Outside scientists as enemies rather than colleagues, no matter how courteous they pretend to be on the surface."

"I'm glad you brought that up," Jack said. "Somehow, I suspect we might not get straight answers to questions of that sort from the Retraining Center, where there's obviously an official line. Just how bad are interspecific relations here, under the surface of calculated courtesy?"

"Not that bad," I assured him. "There are rivalries and prejudices, sure, but the last thing anybody wants is violent conflict. We all know that we're all in the same boat, living on the sufferance of the Larvae. In any kind of conflict, all the Postmortals would lose . . . although it's a matter of opinion whether any genocide carried out by the Larvae could actually count as a victory for anyone. We all do our best to rub along, and ride out any friction. What happened to me really is a very rare occurrence, and occasional violence between vamps and lykes is soon suppressed. The lyke police are fair as well as reasonably efficient, and the ghosts who sit in judgment in the courts are also pretty even-handed, in spite of their irritating superciliousness."

"I see," he said, looking at my wrist again. After a momentary pause, he added: "The crowding can't be making the problems any easier. I seem to remember something from before about the necessity of building a second Reservation, and even a third."

"So I hear," I said. "I suppose it was always a matter of when, rather than if, given that the importation rate into the Ghetto has always been in excess of the redeath rate, but the population density here isn't critical yet, and the new reservation should be complete before it reaches boiling point."

"As long as the trains keep running."

"Obviously—but I see no reason why they would stop. It wouldn't be in anyone's interest, and now that biosynthesis has replaced the traditional methods of supplying the vamps and the zombies from Outside it's difficult to see any reason for shortages to develop."

"You're quite the optimist, aren't you, Peter?"

"Peterkin," I corrected him. "It was probably a nickname, but it's what I remembered after the transition, just as you remember Jack instead of John. And yes, I do try to look on the bright side. I think it makes afterlife more enjoyable. Maybe I'm overcompensating for my Larval self having been a worrier, but I think of it as being sensible and rational."

"Maybe your Larval self was a worrier," said Jack, the suggestion apparently having struck a chord. "I strongly suspect that mine was—it's not uncommon among the Larval, I understand. I admire your calmness, though, and I hope I can learn to share it . . . but you must have been hellishly scared before you managed to undo that wire round your wrist."

"Absolutely terrified," I said. "But as you can see, the old skellies' tales about being scared to life have no substance to them."

He laughed at the weak joke. "Well," he said, "I'm glad you're all right, and thanks for the advice." He stood up as he spoke.

"You're welcome," I assured him. "If you need any more inside dope that the retraining program leaves diplomatically uncovered, you only have to ask. I'll be here all week, apparently, although I hope to be back in dancing form by next Saturday, and fit for work on the following Monday."

"Good luck with that," he said, as I showed him out.

"See you around," I replied.

5

The next morning, however, when the nurse took the dressing off my left wrist in order to change it, and cleaned away the residue of whatever had been in the poultice, what I'd said to Jack about old the skellies' tale, echoing my previous observation to Dr. Setlow, suddenly didn't seem so hilariously absurd.

In fact, it didn't seem funny at all.

"Oh," said the nurse, obviously puzzled. "That's not supposed to happen."

"You can say that again," I said. "The poultice was supposed to help, not make things worse. I thought it was just a placebo, in fact."

My bones were no longer white where the poultice had been applied, but a dull red, ranging from dirty pink to blackish crimson. Nor, it seemed to me, were they simply discolored. It looked suspiciously to me as if something had started growing on the bones of my hand and lower forearm. Although it was difficult to tell, while it was still not much thicker than a layer of paint, it didn't take that much imagination to wonder whether it might be some kind of material flesh.

I touched the area, gingerly, with one of the phalanges of my right hand. It felt sticky, but none of the red came away on the fingertip; apparently, the intervening layer of virtual flesh was insulating it from actual contact.

The nurse also looked closer. "It might be some kind of fungus," she suggested. "The bandage and the ointment were sterile though."

I resented the subtle suggestion that whatever the goo was, its source must be in my bones or my virtual flesh. On the other hand, I also remembered what I had said to Jack about my calculated optimism perhaps being a reaction to excessive anxiety in my former existence. If that really were the case, I thought, then the existential legacy of that psychological darkness might have been merely repressed, awaiting a trigger to burst forth again, and smash my optimism to smithereens.

I criticized myself for that hypothetical change of mind, sternly—but as Dr. Setlow had pointed out the day before, stress sometimes causes strange thoughts to pop into our head, with no regard to absurdity.

I didn't want anything of that sort to have happened. I didn't want to be the kind of Postmortal who carried forward hidden legacies from his larval stage. I didn't want to be any kind of Postmortal whose lovely white bones could begin turning red. I wanted to be the kind of person that Melissa could love, and that surely had to be a person with clean young bones.

I had first noticed the discoloration, in fact, even before I went to the surgery, on the basal phalanges that were sticking out of the bandage that was holding the poultice in place. I had begun to worry even then, but it wasn't until the dressing actually came off and I had seen the full extent of the problem—or what I thought, at the time, to be its full extent—that panic began to set in.

"Can you scrub it off?" I said to the nurse. "Or bleach it? Or something?"

"Dr. Setlow had better have a look at this," said the nurse, without responding to any of my suggestions.

The doctor was busy with a patient, and I had to sit around and wait for him to finish, so that he could spare me a few minutes between appointments. In the meantime, I asked the nurse: "Have you seen anything like this before?"

She hesitated before saying: "No," in a fashion that seemed rather ominous to me. There was obviously something she wasn't telling me. My panic stepped up a notch.

"You don't seem very sure," I observed hoarsely.

"I am," she assured me, in a firmer voice.

As I've said, I might be a piano-player, but I'm not stupid. I was perfectly capable of putting two and two together and remembering that even three is a crowd. "But you've heard of something similar?" I prompted, anxiously.

"I can't make diagnoses," she said, evasively. "Perhaps it was the poultice that caused it—an allergic reaction of some kind."

"I don't have an immune system," I pointed out. "How can it be an allergic reaction?"

"We don't know, as yet, exactly how far the analogies between virtual flesh and larval flesh extend," she said, sententiously. "We've only been studying the question seriously, with the aid of the insights of modern bio-chemistry and biophysics, for half a century or so, and we don't have access to all the kinds of equipment that researchers on the Outside have, let alone the numbers and the institutional support. It's a miracle that osteo-morphic medicine has come as far as it has, even with the legacy of larval osteopathy to draw upon. The lion's share of research money has always gone to the vampires and the lycanthropes, not just because they're more numerous but because their . . . problems . . . seem more urgent, to the Larvae as well as to them. Even the Ghost Faculty treats us at second-class citizens, deviants rather than kindred, although we're made of the same flesh, bones aside."

"So, if it were something analogous to an allergic reaction," I said, my voice taking on a hint of waspishness, "you wouldn't have a clue how to treat it?"

"I didn't say that," she countered. "You'll have to ask Dr. Setlow, obviously, but . . ." She stopped.

"But what?"

She shook her head. "It's not my place, and I'm not qualified. Ask Dr. Setlow."

"Ask me what?" said the doctor, coming through the door at that moment.

I held up my ruddy wrist.

"Ah," he said. "I see." But he said "I see" like the proverbial blind man, who couldn't see at all.

The osteopath examined the wrist very carefully. Then he examined the poultice, with equal care. "It's just a cold compress with a touch of anesthetic," he said. "It was supposed to take a little of the heat out of the bruise on the bone, and soothe the neural transitions at the histological interface. It shouldn't have done that. It couldn't have done that."

"I thought it might be an allergic reaction," the nurse put in, trying to be helpful.

"Bone marrow doesn't produce histamine," said the doctor. "Bone and cartilage are living tissues, so they're not completely inert, in a purely material sense, but that's not a reaction I've ever seen before."

"But you've heard of something similar?" I suggested.

"Why?" he snapped. "What have you heard?"

"Nothing," I told him, not wanting to suggest that the nurse's uncertainty had fallen on to my toe like a dropped clanger. "But if it's not entirely new, there must have been some mention of it, mustn't there? Doctors do swap information, don't they?"

He didn't answer. "It wasn't the poultice," he said, as if he were talking to himself. "The dressing was just covering it up. It's the bone, or some kind of metamorphic reaction or regression in the virtual flesh. Except that . . . I suppose it might have borrowed organic matter from the poultice. If not . . . damn!"

He set about examining the rest of the forearm, and then moved on to my face. "Did you have a shower this morning?" He asked.

"Yes, and I cleaned my teeth too."

"Good, good. No need to panic."

"I'm not panicking," I lied, although I had a horrible sensation that he was still talking to himself, and that the advice was intended for him. That seemed far more ominous, somehow, than if it had been addressed to me. "You're expecting it to get worse aren't you?" I added. "You think it might spread."

"Let's not get ahead of ourselves," he said. "Let's give it another day. It might be nothing; even if it's not nothing, it might be trivial. We won't renew the poultice, or do anything drastic—we'll let the injury rest, and hope that it fades. I've got to see another patient now, so I can't chat any longer, but I'll clear you a thirty-minute appointment tomorrow morning. Ten o'clock?"

"Fine. But . . ."

"No buts . . . at least, not yet. Try not to worry."

"After that?" I complained. "You expect me not to worry, after *that*?"

"Yes I do," he said. "There'll be time to worry if any further symptoms emerge. Until then, there's no reason not to be optimistic. Until ten a.m., then."

And with that, he was gone.

I looked at the nurse. "You wouldn't care to give me a hint as to what it is you think might be wrong with me, I suppose?" I said, knowing full well what the answer would be.

"I honestly don't know," she said, "and if I did, it wouldn't be my place."

She didn't tell me not to worry, though. I didn't know whether to take that as a worrying sign or not.

All the way home I kept peering at my wrist at least once a minute, trying to gauge whether the discoloration of the bone was getting worse, or whether the substance that had apparently been added to it was getting any thicker.

But it's impossible, I told myself, relentlessly. *Larval flesh doesn't regenerate, and even if it could, the process couldn't be triggered by fear. People cannot be scared to life. The saying is just a silly joke, an inversion of what Larvae say when they talk about being scared to death. It's just wordplay. The fact that a crazy thought popped into my virtual brain as that bloody train bore down on me is just a coincidence. It wasn't a presentiment.*

All of which was manifestly true, but it didn't help in the least to stop me worrying.

And that was just the beginning.

The possibility that the mysterious growth was just some sort of limited side-effect of the poultice that Dr. Setlow had applied, allergic or otherwise, didn't take long to disappear. By two o'clock in the afternoon, I could see, beyond the shadow of a doubt, that it was starting on my other hand, as well as traveling up the left arm, all the way up to the elbow. I was already visualizing the possibility of turning red from top to toe—and not a bright red, either, but a dingy red, like clotted blood.

The extra layer on the bones of my left wrist now seemed spongy rather than sticky. It still didn't come away when I touched it, but I soon realized that that wasn't a good sign if I hoped to remove it by washing.

I tried. I tried alcohol as well as water. I tried bleach too. Nothing worked, although the bleach stung, in a way that I had never known bleach to sting before. If I really was growing new flesh, I was obviously developing new capacities for feeling pain along with it. What next? How long would it be before I started feeling hungry? But that, at least, was too absurd, for the moment.

As soon as I was certain that the disease was spreading further, I stationed myself in the bathroom, and looked at myself very intently in the mirror. At first, there was nothing visible—but not for long. It became obvious soon enough that it was beginning to manifest itself on my face, too. There was a rosy flush on my cheeks, and a distinct fuzz on my chin.

It's really happening! I thought. *I really did manage to scare myself to life. I'm regressing to my Larval stage!*

As Dr. Setlow had observed, stress has strange effects.

It was all nonsense, of course. I was still telling myself that. Time could not be made to run backwards. No one—except for the occasional Larval Elixir-of-Life addict—ever grew younger. Even Larval Elixir-of-Life addicts didn't grow younger for long, inevitably falling victim soon enough to their lack of moderation.

My next impulse was to rush back to Dr. Setlow's in search of additional treatment. The credit I'd had to sacrifice just for the stupid poultice had left my bank balance on the slender side, but that wasn't what stopped me—it was the thought that I'd have to go out into the street to get there. That wouldn't have mattered much if I'd only had to go down Winding Sheet Street across the railway and into the heart of zombietown, but in order to reach the surgery I'd have to go up the hill, and once I got to the main road, if not before, I'd be absolutely certain to bump into bony folk by the dozen—and how could I possibly look them in the eye sockets if I'd actually begun to grow *eyes?*

There are some things that simply cannot be exposed to the virtual sight of decent skellies.

What made the prospect seem ten times worse was the admittedly slim possibility that one of the bony folk I bumped if I went out might be Melissa or Salome. I didn't know which would be worse: Melissa looking at me fondly, and her fondness turning to horror as she realized that something was growing on me, or Salome seeking out her friends with the hasty enthusiasm of a girl in possession of hot gossip, to say: "You'll never guess what happened! I met Peterkin the piano-player on the hill, and he looked *disgusting!*"

I didn't actually look disgusting *yet*—just a little *off-color*—but I knew that it was only a matter of time.

I couldn't go out; but that awareness gave birth to an even more horrid thought. Was I condemned to wait in the house, alone—too frightened and ashamed to step outside the door—while I underwent a slow but inexorable metamorphosis into a *Larva*? Was I doomed to emerge from hiding, in the fullness of time, as a horrid pulpy thing with *entrails*, driven by crude appetites, racked by thirst and hunger? And if I did, would I be able to outrun the local zombies the way that a healthy Larval person would have been able to do, or would I be caught and dragged down, perhaps to become the focal point of a feeding frenzy?

Compared with all that, the thought of being shattered and smashed by a railway locomotive seemed a trivial anxiety, hardly worth a shudder.

There was, of course, one obvious way to tackle the immediate problem: put on some clothes.

Bony folk don't like to wear clothing, but we do it readily enough if the necessity arises. In the olden days, I understand, before all of so-called monsterkind was herded into the so-called protective custody of the Reservation, we used to wrap ourselves up routinely in voluminous cowled cloaks in order to hide from the Larval, and every skelly still kept a hooded cloak in his closet, just in case.

In the days before history recognized our real existence, so contemporary legend has it, we must have been in service with the Larval, working the land to produce food that we didn't need and couldn't eat—which is why, according to the sentimental idiots in our ranks, old family portraits often showed our ancestors carrying scythes.

The real reason for that standardized imagery, of course, is that the scythes are symbolic. We were imagined by the Larvae to be personifications of Death, and the scythes were intended to harvest souls. Ever complimentary to the power of their imagination, the smugger Larvae always imagined that they had invented us, just as they pretended that vulgar superstition had invented ghosts, vampires and werewolves, when it hadn't. How vulgar superstition must have laughed when the time finally came for it to be able to say: "I told you so."

Except that that time had never arrived with regard to the bony folk, because even vulgar superstition had thought that we were symbolic, purely metaphorical and not crudely literal. Even credulous peasants thought they were clever enough to know that fleshless skeletons couldn't really walk among them, let alone carry scythes.

Except that we had walked among them, although we probably didn't carry scythes, even though we would have been perfectly able to do so.

Skellies, it seemed, had always got a distinctly raw deal from fate, at least once the ancient Egyptians had given up making mummies—and if you think about it, embalming us in bitumen and wrapping us in bandages qualifies as something of a raw deal in itself. The real raw deals, however, were deep interment and cremation. How many potential Postmortals were thwarted by those practices? Tens of thousands? Millions? Who can tell?

If it hadn't been for crypts, and the occasional adventurous death in exotic circumstances, we could have become extinct for centuries, and probably did, in much of Western Europe. But extinction isn't the end for post-mortalkind, any more than larval death is. As long as the Larvae existed, we could always come back, and we always did. It took us a while, even after the existence of our fellow "monsters" had been formally acknowledged, but we did it. We remain a minority, even by the meager standards of vampires and zombies, but we did it.

Some people, of course, not all of them ghosts, think of us as simply soiled ghosts, who didn't make it all the way to complete virtuality, but we don't see it that way at all. As I said before, moderation is our watchword, and if our forebears had ever had a coat-of-arms, *In medio stat virtus* would have been their motto. Virtue is in the middle, neither in the living flesh nor its absence, but in the bare and beautiful bones, supported by the mystery of virtual flesh. In our view, we, not ghosts, are the true humans, the imagoes of benevolent destiny. And we have long cast aside the shameful cloaks under which we were once compelled to hide our beauty . . .

Except that we still keep them in our closets, just in case. We still keep them, but every time we take them out and put them on, we feel shame.

Which is why simply putting on a garment of some kind in order to go out was not really a simple matter for me, and was something that I was very reluctant to do.

Would it have been better to have lived in the olden days? I wondered, as I stared at my pink-tinged cheeks, reflected in the mirror, in utter horror. *Surely it must have been preferable to living on the next block to delinquent teenage zombies. What do bony folk need civilization for, when all's said and done? Civilization is a larval thing, really.*

Civilization is, in essence, the product of two needs: the need for water and the need to multiply food supplies. Skellies don't eat and they don't drink. Their virtual flesh draws all the nourishment it needs from the cocktail of vapors and gases contained in ambient air, by superficial absorption, although we still have virtual lungs for the purposes of virtual speech—virtual lungs that draw in and expel real air, for the purpose of making ourselves audible even to real ears. But skellies don't need civilization. We do *not* need to be imprisoned in a City. The only train of any relevance to us is the milk train, and only because some of us like to bathe in it. (Forget those old stories about some of us also liking to bathe in blood—those are just fireside tales.) One doesn't need civilization in order to dance, although its artifices do, admittedly, add to the potential elegance of dancing, to some degree.

But I'm digressing again. To return to the point, even the thought of going out in a cloak seemed to be too much to bear for the moment, on that Monday afternoon, as I stared into the mirror, transfixed by horror.

Perhaps it'll go away of its own accord, I thought. *After all, I didn't actually get run over and shattered into a thousand bone shards. I'm not scared any more. I'll be back to normal in no time.*

Then the doorbell rang, and I felt a terrible chill in the marrow of my humeri and femurs.

6

I crept toward the door of the apartment furtively, hoping with all my might that whoever it was might go away. I'd never had occasion before to hope that a ring of the doorbell might be imbecilic zombie teens playing silly games, but that suddenly seemed to be an exceedingly attractive possibility.

The bell rang for a second time—and, after a pause, a third.

"Come on, Peterkin," a voice said. "I know you're in there. I heard what happened."

The chill in my marrow grew worse, and I felt sick from my occiput to my metatarsals. It was Melissa.

I felt that I could easily melt with shame.

It wasn't at all surprising that the news of the injury I'd sustained as a result of the zombie attack had got around, spreading inexorably through the skelly community. It had been nearly twenty-four hours since Jack from number 225 had called round, so the news had had plenty of time to reach Popular Gardens.

"Open the door, Peterkin," Melissa said. "I just want to see how you are—to make sure you're all right."

To say that I was in a quandary was the understatement of the century. If I refused to let her in, she would go away feeling snubbed, feeling that I had deliberately turned her away, and any chance there might have been of building the kind of relationship with her that I wanted to build would be shattered, perhaps forever. But if I let her in, she would see the bloody stains, and then . . .

It seemed to me that Scylla and Charybdis had nothing on those two alternatives, and that there was no middle course to be steered between them, no possible *in medio stat virtus*.

"I can't," I whimpered, not really knowing whether I wanted her to hear me or not, but loudly enough.

"Why not? Your wrist can't be *that* bad."

"I just can't," I said.

"Of course you can. Didn't we have a good time at the Palais on Saturday night? I'm your friend, aren't I? Or have you got that little slut Salome in there?"

"No!" I protested, my voice rising in alarm, as it suddenly seemed that things were getting even worse. "I'm just sick, that's all."

Melissa's voice softened as mine grew harsher. "I know you're sick, Peterkin," she said. "That's why I'm here."

"I mean *really* sick," I said, desperately. "It's not my wrist—it's something else. It might be catching."

"You're a skelly, Peterkin," she said, although I didn't really need reminding. "We don't get sick. We break occasionally, but we don't get *diseases*. Only fleshy folk get diseases."

"Well, I *am* sick," I said. "Not just diseased—disfigured. It's horrible. You *are* my friend, and that's why I can't let you in. I can't let you see me like this."

Somehow, my innate honesty had brought me round to the truth—but I knew, even as the words spilled from my mouth, that the truth wasn't going to do the trick. In fact, I knew as soon as I'd said it that it had probably been a mistake, that it would only increase her determination to win the argument and get into the apartment. But what else could I have said?

"Oh, don't be silly, Peterkin," Melissa said, attempting yet another tone of voice in search of the one that would break down my resistance. "It can't be anything like as bad as you imagine, and I honestly don't mind. *Please* let me in. I'd feel just terrible if you sent me away."

I was in such an awful state of mind that I actually thought that it might serve her right if she *did* see me, and was so horrorstruck that she wouldn't ever be able to look at me again, even if I were to get better. Then I accused myself of being horribly cruel for thinking such a dreadful thing.

Somehow, while I was still figuring out how to defend myself against the charge, my arm made its own decision.

"Don't say I didn't warn you," I said, as my rebel limb opened the door.

She didn't come in immediately, She stood on the doorstep and looked at me long and hard while I tried not to cover my face or run away and hide in the bathroom. Her expression was unreadable.

Eventually, she said "Wow." She said it softly, as if it weren't an exclamation at all, let alone an exclamation of horror and disgust. I wondered whether I might already have melted with embarrassment and gone to the mythical skelly hell from whose bourn no one ever returns.

"Do you still want to come in?" I mumbled.

"Yes, of course," she said, moving past me into the sitting room. "What *is* that stuff, Peterkin? Why have you smeared yourself with it? Did the osteopath give it to you? Why is it on your face and your other arm?"

She sat down on the sofa, but I didn't dare sit beside her. I lowered myself into the armchair.

"I haven't smeared myself," I told her. "It's *growing*. I think it's . . . flesh."

"Flesh?" she repeated, incredulously.

I was tempted to tell her that I thought I'd scared myself to life, but it would have sounded too silly, and I still didn't want to seem silly in her eyes, even if all hope of a meaningful relationship was now utterly lost. How else could I explain it, though? As she'd already observed, bony folk aren't supposed to get sick. It's one of the privileges of the condition. We are, as they say, *immune to all the natural shocks that flesh is heir to.* I said nothing.

It's sometimes difficult for a skelly to look miserable, but another skelly can usually tell. Virtual sight has its intuitions.

"Oh, Peterkin," Melissa said, her voice becoming softer still. "I'm sure it's nothing to worry about. It's hardly noticeable."

"Not *yet*," I murmured.

"Well, that's all the more reason to take it to Dr. Setlow now," she said, very reasonably. "Whatever it is, it's probably best caught early. He'll know what to do. Don't worry about the bill—you'll get it sorted, even if you're in the red for a month or two." The last phrase seemed to me to be particularly ill chosen, but she didn't seem to notice what she'd said.

"I can't," I said. "I just can't."

"That's what you said about opening the door," she retorted. "Put a cloak on, if you like. I'll go with you. If I'm not ashamed to be seen with you, there's not the slightest reason why you should be ashamed to be seen, is there?"

I supposed not—but it wasn't as simple as that. "I saw Dr. Setlow this morning," I confessed. "It was only on my injured wrist then, but he looked elsewhere, including my face. He must have known that this was going to happen, but he wouldn't tell me. It's serious, I know it is."

"Well, it's good that he knows what it is, isn't it?" said Melissa, full of common sense. "If he knows what it is, he'll know what to do about it, won't he?"

"That's not the impression he gave me," I told her. "Quite the opposite, in fact. It seemed to be a prospect that alarmed him. I think this has happened before, and that the outcome wasn't good. I don't want you to be in danger, Melissa. If this is catching, I don't want you to risk catching it."

She sat for a moment or two, considering the implications of that statement, and the fact that I'd made it. Eventually, she said: "What you're saying is that you think it might be fatal?"

I suddenly felt an absurd urge to laugh. Stress does strange things. "I think I'm more afraid of the opposite," I said.

She was a smart girl. "You think you're going back to life?" she said, incredulously.

"Perhaps," I said "Not all entities of material flesh are Larvae."

"You think you might be turning into a zombie? You think this is some kind of metamorphosis, like the one that overcomes lycanthropes at the full moon?"

"Perhaps," I repeated.

She studied my face, and obviously decided that it didn't look that bad—not bad enough, at any rate, to justify my level of panic.

"You don't think," she suggested, diplomatically, "that you might be letting your imagination run away with you?"

"Of course I am," I replied, trying desperately not to snap. "I've never known it to run so fast and so far—but I don't have a brake with which to slow it down."

I realized, at that moment, how genuinely fond of me she must be. Anyone else, I thought—Salome, for certain—would have cut and run. They would have decided that, even if I were letting my imagination run away with me, it was simply not worth the risk of being in my company. In order to continue sitting where Melissa was sitting, she had to like me, a lot.

At any other moment of my afterlife, that would have been the best realization imaginable, but I knew how genuinely fond of her I was because I realized, too, that what I had said had been absolutely true. I didn't want her to run any risk of catching it. I wanted her to be safe.

"Well," she said, "we need to find out what Dr. Setlow knows. We need to find out what this is, and what the outcome of the other cases was, if there have been any. And we need to make sure that he doesn't fob you off with vague evasions. I'll go with you. Sometimes you're a little shy, but if I'm with you, you won't want to show any weakness, will you? You'll insist."

My mouth was probably agape with amazement, not least because she's said "we" three times, as if to insist that we were in it together. I managed to say "I don't . . ." before she cut me off.

"You don't have an appointment," she finished for me, although that hadn't been what I was going to say. "It doesn't matter. It's an emergency. But I'll ring him anyway, just to warn him that we're on our way over."

And that was exactly what she did. She went to the phone, and dialed a number that she obviously knew by heart, and told the receptionist that there was a medical emergency and that she was bringing me to the surgery right away.

I couldn't hear what the receptionist said, but it didn't really matter, because Melissa, having spoken, put the phone down, without bothering to listen to any objections there might have been.

She had always seemed to me to be a trifle shy herself, but either the impression had been mistaken or she was capable of rising to an occasion.

I didn't put up any further resistance, realizing that she was presently irresistible. She'd got me to open the door, and she was determined to take me back to the osteopath's. I really didn't have a choice.

I put on a cloak—one with a very voluminous hood. It was old, dusty and moth-eaten, and I could see that Melissa would rather I hadn't bothered, but she'd already declared that she wasn't ashamed to be seen with me, so that, at least, she felt forced to tolerate. She walked beside me all the way to Dr. Setlow's consulting room, holding her head high, as if she were defying anyone to stare at us.

The zombie brothers were back on the street again, but they hurried off in the opposite direction as soon as they saw me. I hadn't known that zombies could move that fast. Apparently, they too were ashamed of themselves.

I'd expected to have to wait in the general waiting area, or at best to be taken into the nurse's office until Dr. Setlow had finished with his current patient, but his last scheduled appointment must have been some time before, because he seemed to be there on his own, except for the receptionist. He came out to meet us, and then took me into the consulting room, after asking Melissa to take a seat in the waiting-area—which she consented to do, reluctantly.

I disrobed, and showed him the slowly spreading blight. I expected him to be shocked, but he wasn't. I got the impression that he hadn't actually seen it before, but that he'd definitely heard mention of it . . . and perhaps had hoped desperately that he would never have to confront a case personally.

"Oh dear," he muttered. "Dear oh dear."

"How bad is it, Doc?" I asked, keeping my voice as level as I could.

"I don't know," he said. "It's outside my competence. You're a smart fellow, Peterkin—you know what an osteopath does. I deal with breaks, dents and dislocations. To tell you the truth, at least half of my practice is cosmetic, more concerned with the way bones look than actually keeping them healthy and properly articulated. Apart from arthritis, and the occasional bone cancer, I really don't have much to do with diseases, as such, let alone notifiable diseases. This is the first time I've ever . . ."

I cut him off. "Hang on. What do you mean, *notifiable* diseases?"

"It's a legal term. Certain diseases have to be brought to the attention of the relevant authorities. It's almost entirely a zombie matter, usually, given that vampires and theriomorphs seem to have immune systems that are more efficient than the larval, and rumor has it that the notification system is an absolute shambles even in the zombie community, where attitudes to rules and regulations are largely ignored. But still, the regulations exist, and I had to notify your case this morning. The pace of bureaucracy being what it is, they probably wouldn't have got around to contacting you until tomorrow, but . . . well, the long and short of it is that the matter is already out of my hands, as I would have explained to your young lady if she hadn't slammed the phone down on my receptionist."

"Ah," I said. There were several questions crowding my brain, but the one that got to the front of the queue was: "Notify whom?"

"All I have is a phone number, but the code is that of the Communication Center."

"The TV station?"

"No, obviously not the TV station—there are other offices there."

"And what did the person to whom you notified my condition say?"

"Not much. They took your name and address and told me that they'd organize a consultation. I assume that they'll contact you when they've got hold of their consultant, or consultants, and either make an appointment to come to your home or ask you to go to the University."

"The University?"

"That's just a guess. The person I spoke to didn't specify what kind of consultant he meant, but I assume that he meant someone on the Ghost Faculty. That's where the supposed experts on virtual medicine are, and what you seem to have is a . . . an anomalous phenomenon of virtuality."

"Nice jargon," I said. I didn't intend it a compliment. "Look, Doc, I could tell this morning that there was something that your nurse wasn't saying, even before she called you in. It's obvious that you've heard something. If it's just a rumor, you'd hardly be breaking medical confidentiality by passing it on, would you? And if this thing I've got is notifiable, somebody, somewhere, must have seen it before, and must have reason to think that it's cause for concern. At the very least I have to know whether it's contagious. If Melissa's in danger . . . and Jack from 225 . . ."

"I don't know anything for sure," Dr. Setlow assured me, for form's sake, "but I don't think it can be contagious, or the person I spoke to at the CC would have issued some kind of quarantine instructions. As you say, though, the fact that the demand for notification has been issued—and issued recently, only a few weeks ago—must mean that the phenomenon has been observed before, more than once. As for what I've heard . . . well, if you want my opinion, the most significant thing might be what I haven't heard."

"What's that supposed to mean?"

"It means that there aren't that many of us in the City—osteopaths, that is—and even if we don't get together that often, we do talk to one another. If one of us had made a discovery like this, and had initiated the process that had led to the notification, I'd have heard. I don't know whether any of my peers have had to forward a notification, but if they have, it was probably recent, and they were probably asked not to spread the word around—it's not just you who'll get a visit tomorrow morning. But there has been some talk about the notification order, and speculation about the question of where it actually originated from."

"And?" I prompted him.

"And your guess is probably as good as mine—but for what it's worth, I can only think of two possibilities: the Ghost Faculty and Outside."

"Outside? How would anyone on the Outside observe something happening to skellies?"

Actually, that was a silly question, but even if you're smart, you can't be smart all the time. Obviously, skellies don't make the transition from the larval stage instantaneously, or within the walls of the Ghetto. They make it Outside, in morgues, and only get transferred to the Reservation when it's complete. I only had the vaguest idea of how long that usually took, physiologically and bureaucratically, although I did remember the so-called induction that I'd been put through before being transferred to the Ghetto, but it was obvious, after a moment's thought, that larval coroners and their associates had had plenty of opportunity to observe my kind during and immediately after metamorphosis. If what I had was merely a late onset of a disease that normally developed before skellies got shipped off to the Ghetto . . .

I almost asked another stupid question that sprang to mind, but stopped myself just in time. In any case, I'd have had to interrupt Dr. Setlow, who wasn't actually answering my first stupid question, but was at least responding to it, in his own way.

"It's more likely to be the Ghost Faculty, in my opinion," he told me. "They're a secretive lot, and this notification business looks to me like their modus operandi."

"I might not have to wait for the morning, then," I suggested, "or for the doorbell to ring. I'm probably scheduled for a midnight haunting."

"You know better than that, Peterkin," he said, in a mildly critical tone. "This is the twenty-first century—and midnight hauntings are the stuff of larval folktales."

"And ghosts, of course, never make wisecracks about us, do they?" I countered. Actually, I wasn't sure whether they did or not, because even the humblest ghosts don't talk to other folk much, except for functional exchanges of information, and what they talk about among themselves, only they know for sure. Spiritualist mediums are reputed to be the stuff of larval charlatanry.

Dr. Setlow had apparently had enough. "Put your cloak back on, Peterkin," he said, "and go home. I honestly don't know when you'll be contacted, or by whom, or what they'll want you to do, but whatever it is, it's probably better if you're there when they call. I'm truly sorry that I can't do any more for you myself, but as I said, that's the long and the short of it. Try to reassure your girlfriend, if you can—there's no point in frightening her—but in the meantime . . . well, even though we have no reason to think it might be contagious, you might want to avoid . . . intimate contact."

Chance would be fine thing, I thought, unworthily.

"I'll be careful," I assured him. "Thanks."

"Good luck," he said. "And . . . well, I'm sure you'll be fine, once you're in the hands of people who know what they're doing."

I suspected that the last sentence had started out with a different intention, but had changed direction for diplomatic reasons.

"Thanks," I said, again, as I put my Grim Reaper outfit on, and went back to the waiting area.

"Well?" said Melissa, avid for news.

"It's beyond his remit," I said. "He's called in consultants. They'll contact me at home, tonight or tomorrow. I'll probably have to go to the University for treatment, but as he had to notify someone of my coming down with it, it's obviously familiar to the someone in question, who'll surely know how to treat it." I was doing what I'd been advised to do, and trying to reassure her. It wasn't that easy, though.

"But you're going to be all right?" she demanded, as we walked along the street, going downhill.

"I hope so," I told her. "The Doc says that it's probably not catching, but . . . well, he doesn't know for sure. You might not want to get too close." That was, to say the least, a stupid way of putting it, given that what I was hoping for was that she wanted to get a lot closer than she had to date . . . provided, of course, that she didn't catch anything in the process.

She knew, though, that I was simply concerned, and wasn't trying to drive her away, and I got the impression that she interpreted my concern entirely in my favor.

"I'm not frightened," she assured me.

I had a vague impression of once having read, probably in my larval stage, that fear is a negotiable emotion, that the physiological stimulation it gives to squishy flesh is reinterpretable by squishy minds, if they're in the mood, as erotic attraction. I had no idea whether there was any analogical process applicable to virtual flesh, but I couldn't help hoping that there might be—unworthily, again.

What I said, though, was: "I am—for you as well as for me."

"I know," she said—which wasn't what I'd expected her to say. "But that's why I'm going to keep you company for a while longer, if you don't mind. I don't want to leave you on your own, and as I'm already exposed, it's better if I stay with you than somebody else, don't you think? I can answer your door and keep anyone else away. It's the responsible thing to do, after all."

I hadn't actually thought about it, but when I did, I realized that she had a point. She'd been quick off the mark to call round when she heard about my run-in with the zombie gang, only beaten by Jack because he lived next door, but she probably wouldn't be the last, and in the circumstances, it might indeed be a good idea to have someone to intercept them, lest there be a risk in seeing me, however slight.

It occurred to me, too, given what she'd said about "that slut Salome" that she might have particular reasons to intercept some potential callers, but that only made the prospect seem even more flattering.

"Well," I said, wishing that I could make a better job of feigning reluctance, "If you're sure . . ."

"You'd do the same for me," she said.

To which I couldn't help thinking, unworthily yet again: *Chance would be a fine thing.* But not, of course, because I was wishing misfortune upon her, Almighty Chance forbid.

Then I had a sudden surge of self-pity. *Why me? I thought. Why now? Everything was going so well, on Saturday, and everything would obviously have gone even better thereafter if things had only taken their normal course . . . and I have to come down with some bloody exotic disease, and might even die of it . . . and all Melissa's sympathy will go to waste in tears instead of . . . intimate contact. It's so bloody unfair . . .*

And that was when, from the top end of Winding Sheet Street, I saw that I wasn't going to have to wait for the next morning to be contacted by the people who'd been notified about my condition, or even for midnight.

There was an ambulance parked outside the door of number 227, and two lykes in white coats—I only assumed that they were lykes, of course, but they were very definitely wearing white coats—standing outside it, obviously waiting to take me away.

7

Just as there are jokes in the Ghetto about midnight hauntings that really have no place there, being hangovers from larval life and larval superstition, so there are jokes about men in white coats who come to take you away. They're absurd, because there are no lunatic asylums in the Ghetto, and if there were, they wouldn't be like the lunatic asylums of larval melodrama, in which sadistic doctors torture patients with cold showers and electric shocks.

Even so, such silly clichés are not devoid of psychological effect, and my first reaction, on seeing the ambulance, and the two men in white coats—not to mention the mixed crowd of skellies and zombies, some twenty-five or thirty strong, that had doubtless materialized out of the houses on either side of the street in order to find out what was happening—was to turn round and run.

Why? Where would I have gone? I have no idea. But I do know, even though it was piling absurdity upon absurdity, that the principal reason that I didn't turn and run was that Melissa was beside me, and I didn't want to let myself down in her eyes.

I didn't even hesitate. I just kept on walking, steadily.

To say that I was obvious is the understatement of the century. Even if I'd been *au naturel,* at least some members of the crowd would have recognized me, all the way from 227 to the top of the street, and the word would have gone around. As things were, in my Grim Reaper outfit, it was evident that I was a skelly with something to hide, and it didn't take a genius to connect up the presence of an ambulance and white coats with someone coming down the street wearing a vast hooded cloak. From the moment I turned the corner, all eyes, both squishy and virtual, were fixed on me—and not just thirty pairs of eyes, because there were people at the windows too.

Winding Sheet Street is a long street, but I had never realized quite how long it could seem from the top to the middle, even going downhill.

I think Melissa cursed, but she did it under her breath, so all I heard was a kind of grunt.

If I had stayed at home instead of letting Melissa drag me away to the surgery, I couldn't help thinking, *they could just have come up and rung my doorbell, and whisked me away. Now, it has to be a big show.* Naturally, I didn't blame Melissa, or myself; I blamed the oafs in the ambulance, who obviously had all the diplomatic flair of a brace of polecats.

I eventually got to confront them. I opened my mouth in order to say: *Are you gentlemen looking for me, by any chance?* in a suitably cavalier tone, but I didn't get the chance.

"Are you Peter Strangland, sir?" asked one of the men in the white coats, who definitely wasn't in the running for any prize at all, whether for deduction or diplomacy.

It was a truly astonishing question. I knew, of course, as a matter of information that had been passed on to me, that the name of my Larva had been Peter Strangland, but it wasn't *my* name. My name was Peterkin: the name I had remembered, the name I applied to myself: my skelly name. Nobody in the Ghetto—absolutely nobody, not even a malevolent zombie—would ever have asked me whether my name was "Peter Strangland."

And that was when I realized that the two men in white coats weren't lykes at all. They were sheep in wolves' clothing. They were Larvae. They had come into the Ghetto from Outside.

My tone wasn't at all cavalier as I replied: "Who wants to know?"

He obviously took that as a yes, because he actually had the nerve to look relieved, and I realized that he'd been nervous . . . perhaps very nervous . . . because of the crowd, and perhaps because of the nature of the crowd. As an Outsider, finding himself in the center of a crowd of skellies and zombies must have been an intensely un-nerving experience, no matter what he had been told about the placid security of the Reservation.

"We've been sent to collect you, sir," he said, trying his utmost to sound unctuously polite, and failing. "My name's Henry."

Even at the time, it occurred to me that I didn't have to go, and that if I'd wanted to refuse, the crowd would actually have backed me up, because at least some of them must have deduced, as I had, that the seeming lykes weren't lykes at all, but Larvae. But what would have been the point of refusing? In fact, didn't I have just as much interest as they had, and perhaps more, in going quietly.

"Yes, of course, Henry," I managed to say. "I wasn't expecting . . . you . . . so soon."

The Larva who hadn't spoken had already had the back door of the ambulance open. He was in a hurry. He wanted to get away. The proximity of so many zombies was definitely making him extremely nervous. He'd been expecting skellies, obviously, but not zombies, and not in such numbers.

I climbed inside, meekly. Then Melissa set out to follow me.

The Larva who had spoken to me automatically moved to intercept her. Doubtless he had his orders—but Melissa didn't give a damn about his orders.

"I'm going with Peterkin," she announced, loudly. It wasn't a request, it was a declaration. She didn't look at the crowd, and she didn't make the slightest threatening gesture, but the two ambulance men were obviously scared. They were just there to pick me up. They wanted to get away, as fast as possible, from all the unexpected attention. They didn't want any kind of dispute. The Larva stood aside and let Melissa climb into the back of the ambulance with me."

"This might not . . ." I began—but she cut me off.

"I said I'd stay with you," she said, "and I will." That was it. She'd made up her mind, and sheer obstinacy was pulling her into a situation whose nature and dimensions she couldn't estimate.

The Larva that had spoken to me climbed into the back with us, while the other one closed the door and then went round to the front of the vehicle to climb into the driving seat.

"Where are we going, Henry?" I asked the man who had called me by my larval name, perhaps not even realizing what a gaffe he was committing.

"Not far," he told me. "To a private clinic."

"Not Outside?" I said, just to check.

He looked slightly surprised, as if he hadn't realized that it would be obvious to me and everyone else what he was.

"No, sir," he said. "It's inside the Reservation, near the Communication Center."

"I don't know of any private clinic near the Communication Center," I said. It was a bluff. How would I have known whether there were any private clinics near the Communication Center? But he didn't know that I didn't know.

"It's recent, sir," he said. "Still in the process of organization, in fact."

Deliberately, I tipped my hood back, to display my face. "Because of the epidemic?" I said.

He was just a pick-up man, not a paramedic, but he obviously knew enough to say: "It's not an epidemic, sir. It doesn't seem to be contagious. Dr. Charteris is still trying to identify the cause of the . . . phenomenon, but he's sure that there's no danger in contact. The patients are allowed visitors, twice a day, by appointment." He glanced at Melissa.

"And is Dr. Charteris a Larva too?" I asked, bluntly.

Larvae, of course, don't call themselves Larvae, which is why he replied: "He's human, yes sir," in a slightly resentful tone.

"We're all human," I told him, coldly. "Why is a Larval doctor investigating an osteomorphic condition?"

Again, the Larva seemed surprised by the question. "Dr. Charteris is the world's foremost expert on . . . the osteomorphic condition," he said. "There's no one better qualified to examine it, believe me."

"And no one better qualified to find a cure?" I queried, watching his squashy eyes like a virtual hawk.

"Exactly, sir," he said—but I'd seen him look away for a fraction of a second, evading the question reflexively before providing the tokenistic response.

One man's meat is another man's poison, Larvae are reputed to say—and, more importantly, to think. Which implies that one man's poison might be another man's meat . . . or, to put it another way, one man's disease another man's cure. What I wanted, obviously, was to get rid of the filthy crimson fuzz that had suddenly started growing on my lovely bones, but it occurred to me that the people whom Dr. Setlow had been obliged to notify of my condition might not see it that way. They might think of it as actually *getting better*: if not actually returning to a Larval condition, at least becoming more Larval in appearance.

And Larvae, not osteopaths, or even members of the Ghost Faculty, seemed to be in charge of the mysterious clinic.

There's something distinctly fishy about all this, I thought.

Nobody knows, of course, how many Larvae there might be in the Ghetto, because, unless they make a stupid gaffe like calling a skelly by his Larval name, nobody can tell them apart from theriomorphs merely by sight—except, of course, after dark when there's a full moon. The general opinion, however, is that there are very few, if any. After all, the whole point of the Larvae setting up the so-called Reservation was to isolate what they considered to be monstrous species from their own population. Doubtless some of them did come into the Ghetto occasionally, for various reasons of administration and negotiation, without making themselves obvious—but setting up a clinic was a different matter, and bringing in auxiliary staff from Outside rather than hiring locals was an additional quirk.

Something was going on. Something weird.

After a pause for thought, which seemed longer than it probably was, in terms of objective chronology, I said to the man in the white coat: "I'll be allowed visitors in the clinic, you say?"

We both glanced sideways at Melissa. "Yes, sir, one at a time, by appointment," he said. "The . . . young lady can come to see you if she wishes, between two and four in the afternoon, or five and seven in the evening. All she has to do is telephone to reserve the slot."

"Good," I said. "And if I want to go out?" I didn't think that was likely, but I wanted a more accurate estimate of my status.

"Dr. Charteris doesn't advise it, sir," the Larva said, "but you're a free agent. You're not a prisoner." He knew as well as I did that that was what I wanted to know.

I could have continued the interrogation, but the ambulance was already pulling to a halt. Obviously, we had arrived. Knowing that I only had a few seconds left, I was quick to ask: "Will I be on some sort of ward, with other patients?"

"You'll have a room of your own, for the moment, sir," he said, "but there's a common room where you'll be able to see and talk to the other patients. You'll be able to get a sense of how the process is likely to develop."

I took due note of his use of the word 'process,' instead of disease, as well as taking the inference that there were patients in the mysterious clinic in whom the symptoms were much further advanced than mine, but I also took note of his use of the phrase "for the moment"—which implied that I might not have a room of my own for long, if the disease continued to spread.

The fact that there were cases further advanced than mine, I thought, would at least give me some advance warning of what they and I might be metamorphosing into, and thus provide some indication of exactly what sort of monster I might become, if I couldn't be cured . . . assuming that anyone was actually trying to find a cure. Obviously, if they were, they hadn't found one yet.

The back door of the ambulance opened. Melissa steeped down first, and I followed her. We were in the moderately large courtyard of a fairly plush detached building, which was, indeed, along the road from the Communication Center. It had obviously been designed as some kind of administration center, and had presumably been a hive of bureaucratic activity for most of its fifty- or sixty-year lifespan, before being pressed into medical service.

"There's no need to come in," I said to Melissa, in a low voice. "It was very kind of you to come with me, but you can see that I won't be alone, and you heard the visiting hours, if you'd like to come back. Thanks for everything."

She must have read the pleading expression in my virtual eyes. "I'll definitely come and see you," she assured me. Her voice dropped to a whisper. "Since we're here, I'll call in on Phil. His office is just down the road, and he might have picked up some gossip about *all this*." She waved her hand at the building

The idea of her calling in on flash Phil didn't fill me with delight, but the thought that she might be able to pick up some under-the-table information about what the hell was going on was adequate compensation. I acknowledged her leave-taking with an awkward nod of the head, wishing that it were practical to be a little more demonstrative. She understood. As she moved away, the white-coated Henry escorted me to the imposing portal of the edifice.

It seemed entirely in keeping with the nature of the building that I was ushered into a typically bleak waiting room, asked to take an uninviting seat, and told that someone would collect me in a few minutes.

I wasn't sorry about the interval; it gave me a chance to think. I didn't know how much of the building was actually being used as a clinic for people with my condition, but the suggestion of its dimensions was that if there wasn't an epidemic yet, there soon might be. Clearly, the silly notion that I'd been "scared to life" had to be discarded, but the fact remained that something had happened to trigger the phenomenon. The fact that the mysterious Dr. Charteris didn't think the condition was contagious probably wasn't a cast-iron guarantee, so it was possible that I'd picked it up at the Palais on Saturday. It was even possible, I supposed, that I'd picked it up from the zombies who had given me a hard time afterwards, even though the disease and decay that routinely runs riot in zombie bodies wasn't usually communicable to other species.

On the other hand, it was surely possible that the shock I'd had while tied to the railway line really had been the trigger, and that the old joke about being scared to life might have some kernel of distorted truth behind it. The other sufferers obviously hadn't been wired to a railway track by deranged zombies, but they might have suffered other traumas. But skellies in the Ghetto must have been suffering all sorts of shocks for half a century or more without the phenomenon becoming noticeable until very recently. So what had changed? Perhaps the question wasn't so much *why me?* as *why now?*

The door opened then and someone came in. I felt a genuine wave of relief as I saw that she was a skelly, whose bones proudly displayed the effects of a recent bleach-and-polish. She was obviously a nurse rather than a patient. I felt less isolated by a whole order of magnitude when I realized that I wasn't entirely in Larval hands.

"Peterkin," she said, "I'm Adelaide. I'm sorry that I wasn't here to greet you when you arrived, but we're still in a slight state of confusion. Dr. Charteris can't see you immediately, I'm afraid, but he'll be with you as soon as he can. I'll take you to the common room, so you can meet some of the others. Please don't be alarmed . . . we really are making progress, and there's every reason to be optimistic."

I didn't know her, but I was prepared to believe that she must have the same objective that I and the rest of her patients did. She, at least, must have an accurate idea of the direction in which true optimism lay.

She took me up a flight of stairs to the first floor, and along a short corridor to the left, before opening a door and ushering me into the "common room."

There were four people in the room: two male and two female. Even a Larva could have identified them as two males and two females—that was how far their conditions had progressed. They were carrying between twenty and forty pounds of ugly red flesh apiece, mostly distributed in a fashion that was extremely unflattering. They weren't wearing clothes—they hadn't so much as a dressing-gown between them—but the charged atmosphere suggested that they were having some trouble maintaining that defiant attitude.

I had raised my hood again, reflexively, when I stepped out of the ambulance in the courtyard, but now I pushed it back on to my shoulders, so that my fellow patients could see what was happening to me.

"Why," said one of the males, "it's young Peterkin—the pianist at the school." When I looked at him uncomprehendingly he sighed. "Sorry," he said. "I haven't quite got used to the fact that I'm unrecognizable. I'm Lysander, the fiddle-player with the Carillon of Skulls—we play at the Palais sometimes, and at the Grand Guignol for the saber-dancers, and we do the occasional gig when your star pupils do their party pieces."

Only two weeks had passed since I'd last seen the violinist. The thought immediately flashed into my mind that perhaps *he* was the one who'd passed the disease on to me—but I had to suppose that, if he'd been able to infect me, given that we hadn't actually touched, he'd have given it to everyone else in the Grand Guignol that night, and there had been a good crowd, so I discounted the possibility immediately. The more worrying aspect of his presence was the sight of the flesh he'd put on in a mere fortnight.

"Take a good look, son," said one of the females—the fleshiest of the four. "This time next month, you'll probably be able to pass for a squishy in a dim light. In fact, to all intents and purpose, you'll *be* a squishy. You'll be drinking and eating . . . and even though the more disgusting things are optional, you'll have *hormones* to torment you. The psychiatrist says that even if the worst comes to the worst we'll adjust, in time, but she hasn't managed to convince any of the patients, even with the aid of her ridiculous hypnotherapy. I'm Helen, by the way—no relation to Helen of Troy, so far as I know. Mind you, it'll probably look better on you than it does on me, you having such young bones. Your caterpillar must have died young, as well as recently."

I prickled at the indelicacy of the remark. I couldn't manage a reply.

"It could be worse, lad," the second male said, coming to my rescue. "Better to be turning back into a Larva than some other kind of Postmortal, if that really is what's happening—but there's still plenty of time to find a cure before we get to that pass. At least that quack Charteris has assured us that we can't be turning into zombies! I'm Billy."

Billy didn't seem, to my admittedly untutored eye, to be as far along as his companions; his flesh hadn't yet taken on the same *distinction* as Helen's. It still looked more like undifferentiated goo than functional tissue. There were bare patches on his arms and legs where attempts had been made to scour it away.

He saw me looking at the raw patches, and added: "Yes, I'm the volunteering type—try anything, I will. Once, anyway." He used the phalanges of his left index-finger to point to his right forearm. "This here's straight-forward scraping—hurts like hell, and the effect hardly lasts an hour." He pointed at his left leg with the same finger. "This is sulfuric acid," he said. "Same problem, and it also turns good calcined bone to something more like translucent plastic. The other leg's quicklime—just as painful, and it takes all the spring out of the con-nective sinews. Helen, Lysy, Jill and a few of the guys upstairs have tried some of the same things, and a few others besides, but we're running out of options. You look like a sensible lad who'll take other people's word for things, though—wish I was! Don't let them try any-thing crazy on you."

"Crazy's all we have left to try," the other female said. "Mind you, doing nothing at all's no better than scrubbing away with wire wool once the itching starts. I thought I knew what an itch was before, but until you've felt flesh itch you haven't really lived. Joke. My name's Jillian, by the way, not Jill, although it does start with a J. I've haven't been here very long —in the City, that is—and nor has Lysander, but it isn't our being such new entrants that causes the problem, because Billy's been here decades."

"I'm right, though, aren't I?" Helen said, picking up the thread. "Your bones are a lot younger than those the rest of us have, which might mean that they're strong enough to beat this thing, if any bones can. Piano player, are you? That's good. Do you think you can get us a piano, Doc? Young Peterkin can help Lysander to enter-tain us, when the depression gets too much to bear."

It wasn't until she said "Doc" that I realized that some-one else had now come in behind me. I turned round, to find myself looking a fully fledged Larva in the face. He seemed to me to be about fifty years old, and might have been distinguished, or even handsome, by Larval stan-dards. He wasn't wearing a white coat, but he was fully dressed, in a gray suit that was probably quite expensive, with a gleaming white shirt and an actual cravat.

"Dr. Charteris, I presume," I said.

"That's correct," he replied. "Leopold Charteris. Peterkin, isn't it? I just wanted to come and say hello. I'll leave you with these good people for a few more min-utes, if you don't mind. Adelaide will come to collect you when I have time for a proper initial consultation, and she'll show you to your room afterwards. Please excuse me, for the moment."

And he left again.

"You've hurt your wrist," Lysander observed, having inspected the place where the "phenomenon" had first made itself manifest. "Have you already tried one of Billy's drastic measures?"

"No," I said, "this was before, not after. I had an un-fortunate encounter on Saturday night with a zombie gang. On Sunday morning Dr. Setlow put a poultice on it, and when the nurse wanted to change the dressing this morning . . . well, I didn't know whether to blame the zombies, or the poultice, or neither."

"Probably neither," opined Helen. "Setlow's a quack too, but at least he observes the Hippocratic principle of doing no harm, which is more than I can say for Charteris. The poultice won't have started it. As for zom-bies, I don't think any of the rest of us have been within spitting distance of one."

"And there are no common factors between the four of you to provide any kind of hint as to the trigger?" I queried.

"Sorry, lad," Lysander said. "There are two more of us, so you make seven, and we've all been racking our virtual brains trying to find something we have in common, as you can imagine, without success. I was tempted to blame a combination of premature world-weariness and incipient arthritis in my old bones, but the others won't even admit to world-weariness."

"No way," said Billy. "I'm nowhere near ready to throw in the towel, even now. If I have to walk through fire, I'll try it."

"Oh, hush, Billy," Jillian said. "What did the zombies actually do to you, Peterkin?"

"Wired me to the railway track when the last cross-town passenger train was due," I said. I was able to speak laconically about it now that I had something worse to worry about. "I managed to free one wrist just in time to roll out of the way, but this one was still bound to the track—it got wrenched and squeezed when the engine's wheels cut through the wire." I held up my wrist.

"Damn zombies!" said Billy. "Scum of the earth."

"I came down on a Monday too," Helen observed. "You weren't at the Palais Saturday night, by any chance?"

"Of course he was," Jillian said, before I could even nod my head. "We were all out somewhere, the weekend before we started showing, at the Guignol or the Field of Frolic if not the Palais—along with at least seven or eight hundred other people. If we'd picked it up there, or if dancing were enough to set it off, *everybody* would have come down with it. There'd be no bony folk left."

"So why us?" said Lysander, mournfully. "Why us?"

"That's not the point," said Billy. "The point is, what are we going to *do* about it. And I mean *us*, because Charteris isn't even trying, if you ask me. He's let me try all sorts of things, and monitored the results with avid attention, but I get the distinct impression that he wasn't in the least disappointed when they didn't work. He's fascinated by what's happening, but his first priority is to track it, not to stop it."

"The shrink from the Ghost Faculty is no better," Jillian put in. "Nobody can read a ghost's expression, but you know what they're like. They think bones are disgusting, so superfluous flesh just seems to them to be more of the same. She didn't care. Like Charteris, she might be fascinated, but she'd rather try to delve around in our memories of past lives than actually help us. The City osteopaths might be just bone-setters, but surely they ought to be in charge here. Who actually appointed this Charteris fellow?"

"Outsiders, obviously," said Lysander. "They pretend that we run our own affairs in the Ghetto, but that's only on their sufferance. As soon as anything happens that interests them, they show their hand and step in—with cravats and white coats, no less! What can they be thinking?"

"That's a good question," I put in, seeing my chance. "Why do they care? What the hell does it have to do with the Larvae? It seems to me that there's something deeply fishy about this set-up."

I saw immediately that I'd committed a slight gaffe. They exchanged glances, and moved their eyes from side to side expressively. They'd already decided that that was indeed the crucial question, that there was indeed something fishy about the set-up, but also that it might not be diplomatic to ponder it too loudly, in case the hypotheses that they voiced caused excessive offense. Clearly, they thought that the common room walls might have virtual ears. It occurred to me that they might simply be being paranoid—but the logical corollary to that judgment was that they might not.

"We shouldn't be sounding off like this in front of poor Peterkin," Jillian opined. "He's only just got here. We should be helping him to feel at home."

"It's fine," I hastened to say. "Obviously, I wouldn't wish this on anybody else, but there is a certain relief in knowing that I'm not alone."

"We all feel that," Lysander agreed, "or did at first. But two's company and seven's a crowd. It isn't going to stop, is it? No matter what triggered it, it's not going to stop with us. Jill's right—we're all going to come down with it. We're a species threatened with extinction."

"That's not . . ." Jillian began, but she wasn't allowed to finish denying that she'd been issuing a prediction.

"And what are they going to do about it," Helen interjected, bitterly, "apart from bringing in ghost shrinks to assure us that what's happening to us isn't as bad as we think and teach us to meditate? It's only a matter of time before they start a retraining program . . . not that the Larvae would let us back into their ranks even if we wanted to join them. Whatever becomes of us, in their eyes we'll just be one more set of freaks in the Ghetto."

I could tell by the way that Lysander looked shiftily sideways again that not only had the idea already crossed his mind, but that he could see corollaries that he didn't want to voice. I was beginning to see possibilities myself with which I didn't want my imagination to run away . . . at least, not yet.

Helen wasn't about to stop, though. She frowned—*actually* frowned—and said: "What *they*'ll tell us, Peterkin, is that we aren't sick at all. *They*'ll say we're *getting better*. They'll never be able to understand that once you've joined the bony folk, you never want to go back."

I was uncomfortably reminded of the zombie teen's resentful allegation that skellies thought they were a cut above everybody else. Perhaps, I thought, this was a judgment on me for pusillanimously trying to deny the fact.

"But if we're just the tip of an impending iceberg," I murmured, as much to myself as to my new friends, "something needs to be done about it, before it's too late."

"Damn right," said Billy. "Don't think we haven't been trying, lad. Already too late for us, I dare say—but maybe not for you. At least we're learning more every day." The way he pronounced the final sentence suggested that he didn't believe it. I realized the awful absurdity of the fact that a skelly who'd spent the last few days allowing himself—positively demanding, no doubt—to be scraped with butchers' knives and scrubbed with all manner of chemical reagents was actually trying to reassure me, altruistically desirous of keeping my spirits up.

"Lysander could be wrong," Jillian pointed out, scrupulously. "We don't know that it's going to spread even to a substantial fraction of the population, let alone threaten to become general. We might just be unlucky, a mere handful of individuals who aren't immune."

"Or we might just be unlucky in being at the head of the queue," retorted Lysander. "Maybe it's just gathering its strength by picking us off one by one? Maybe it's just playing with us while it makes its preparations for the big push, when it can wipe us all out at its leisure, savoring every moment?"

He was looking at me. Virtual eyes don't wink, but his could, even though they weren't fully formed yet, by a long way.

I couldn't be entirely sure, but I took the inference that he was trying to suggest to me, without saying so, that when he said "it" he really meant "they": that what was happening to the five of us, and the two I hadn't yet seen, might not be a bizarre coincidence at all, but enemy action.

My first thought was that he was definitely being paranoid . . . but my second was that he just might be right. Perhaps, in fact, I might have been deliberately infected. If so, it surely couldn't have been the zombies. It could have been a touch at the Palais, during one of the line-dances . . . or perhaps my very first thought had been correct, and Dr. Setlow's poultice . . .

I cut off that line of thought. It wasn't something I wanted to think about, let alone voice.

But the question remained: Why were the Larvae interested? Why was Dr. Leopold Charteris in charge of the clinic, not an osteopath or a representative of the Ghost Faculty? After all, Helen was surely right. Even if some or all of us did put on sufficient squishy flesh to pass for Larvae, they weren't going to throw us a party to welcome us back to the Outside world, were they?

In the meantime, Jillian said: "Don't be melodramatic, Lysander. Seven cases don't presage a pandemic. And if it does spread, you can be sure that the response will escalate. Every osteopath in the city will be working on it, if they aren't already . . ."

I was pretty sure that they weren't already, having seen Dr. Setlow only an hour or two before, but the general paranoia was sufficiently catching for me not even to think about anything so touchy out loud.

The growing tension was broken then, when the door to the common room opened and Nurse Adelaide—the lovely, spick-and-span, utterly reassuring Nurse Adelaide—came in to say: "Dr. Charteris is ready for your first consultation now, Peterkin. Please come this way."

I was surprised to discover that I had an odd mixture of conflicting feelings in response to that invitation. A part of me wanted to get out of that panic-stricken atmosphere, but another part of me wanted to continue the crazy conversation, and seek out yet more reasons for turning confusion into terror. Even though Melissa was no longer there, though, I wanted to keep up the act of being in control, of taking everything in my heroic stride.

I went with Nurse Adelaide, meekly, therefore, and I sat down in a leather armchair opposite Dr. Leopold Charteris, as casually as I could, trying to imply that I was the kind of skelly who could confront a Larva without feeling the slightest intimidation or disgust.

8

"I'm sorry for the delay, Peter," said the Larval doctor, "but we're under pressure here, as you can see. We had rather hoped that the phenomenon might be so rare as to be prodigious, but your case makes seven in fairly rapid succession, and we're now afraid that the snowball might become an avalanche. If it does . . . well, it's not just our calculations of probability that will be thrown out completely. The Ghost Faculty has also been taken completely by surprise."

For a second, annoyed by the mistake he'd made in calling me by my name, I thought about throwing caution to the winds and simply asking him *the* question, but I decided against it. I already knew what his answer would have to be, and I didn't imagine for a moment that I'd be able to tell from his reaction to being asked whether he was lying or not. It was better to wait.

Instead, I muttered, "It came as a hell of a surprise to me too."

"Obviously," he said, perhaps trying to sound sympathetic. Perhaps he would have, to another Larva, but to me he simply looked shifty, and I got the strong impression not only that there was a lot that he wasn't telling me, but that he was lying through his teeth. And then, suddenly—rather belatedly, in fact--I realized how odd it was that the hired help who had picked me up from

Winding Sheet Street had not only called me Peter but had added the surname I used to have in my previous existence, and it suddenly occurred to me to wonder how they had both known what my Larval name had been, and why they'd used it.

"You knew!" I blurted. "You knew this was going to happen to me! You bastard! It really is an experiment! You did this to me, didn't you? To all of us!"

So much for it being better to wait.

I'd seen enough Larval TV to be able to judge that he was utterly horrified by the suggestion. "No, no, no!" he said. "You mustn't think that! It's not true! We wouldn't. You have to believe me . . ."

"Why the hell should I?" I snapped back at him. "Nobody's telling us anything! Why shouldn't we think, in the absence of any other plausible hypothesis, that this is being done to us deliberately . . . and who else can we suspect, if not you?"

"Please!" he said, "I really am on your side. I know I'm not postmortal, but I really am America's foremost expert on postmortal medicine, with special reference to osteomorphism. You mustn't think that I'm your enemy, let alone that I would do something like . . . what you just accused me of doing. I would never . . ."

He actually had to stop, to catch his breath and collect himself. I wasn't at all sure that watching the shows on TV that the larval censors thought fit for postmortal consumption really gave Ghetto-dwellers an accurate notion of larval psychology and emotional expression, but my impression was that he was either sincere or a good actor.

But I also had the very strong impression that I was right—that my impulsive guess, even though it had been based on evidence that might look flimsy seen without the benefit of the paranoia that had just been wound up in the few minutes I'd spent in the common room was correct. My arrival here—or, to be strictly accurate, the arrival here of a skelly whose Larva had been named Peter Strangland—had not been unexpected . . . and of all the bizarre features of the adventure, that was surely the most bizarre of all.

The ball was in his court. He couldn't tell that my virtual eyes were staring at him, unless he was one of the rare Larvae who had unusually good virtual sight and the gift of not allowing its insights to be eclipsed by the information of his material eyes, but he must have realized that my expression was both hostile and demanding.

"This is unfortunate," he murmured, more to himself than me, but he was quick to recover. "But it isn't what you think, Peter . . ."

"Peterkin," I snapped. "I'm *Peterkin*. Not Peter. That was some Larva I can't remember—*not me*."

His expression changed again, and I assumed that he'd belatedly realized the mistake he'd made, and why, although it was stupid, given that he's already called me by my name once, and had presumably imagined that in shortening it for the purpose of the more official consultation he was simply injecting a little formality into the conversation, it wasn't trivial. I was prepared to believe that he was the world's foremost expert on skelly anatomy, metamorphosis and physiology, but he clearly didn't know a damn thing about skelly culture and society.

"Yes, of course," he said. "I'm sorry. But it really isn't what you think. You're right, of course, about my not telling you and the others everything. That's something of which doctors have to be very careful, because communicating hypotheses to patients can so easily influence the development of their conditions. Self-diagnoses via the internet cause so much hypochondria, and even psychosomatic inductions . . ."

"Not to skellies," I told him, coldly. "That's one of the technologies you Larvae are keeping to yourselves." I didn't bother to add that it was a sore point, because I didn't really care, although I knew that there were lykes and vamps who were building up a considerable resentment over the issue.

"The argument applies to any channel of information," he said, swiftly, presumably eager to move on to a region of the argument where he might be able to avoid putting his squishy foot in his squishy mouth every time he opened it. "I'm sorry . . . truly sorry . . . if I've given you and the others a false impression of what I'm trying to achieve by not spelling out precisely enough what lines of inquiry I'm following and what results I'm obtaining. Yes, you're correct, I *had* formed a hypothesis that you might be affected by the syndrome—but not, God forbid, because I did anything to produce it, or had any reason to suspect someone else of doing something to produce it. Please, you have to believe me."

I didn't think I did have to believe him, but I thought that at least I had to hear him out. "What hypothesis?" I demanded. "Why did you single me out as someone who might be affected? How can it possibly have anything to do with my larval self?"

I think he looked slightly surprised that I'd made that deduction, although it seemed obvious enough, but his reaction was complicated, and I might have been misreading it. "What makes you think that what's happened to you has anything to do with your mortal experience?" he asked.

"I don't," I told him. "But you obviously do?"

He was still confused. "Why do you think that?" he asked.

"Partly because you just called me Peter," I told him, "but mainly because the white-coated moron you sent to make a public exhibition of wheeling me away not only made the same mistake but added the surname that Peter used to have, when he existed. Obviously, you have some way of looking that up, on this internet thing that you Outsiders have, so you presumably did, the moment Dr. Setlow notified you that I'd been infected—but if you're using my old self's name between yourselves, instead of my real name, it must be because you think it's significant in some way. I may only be a piano-player in a school, but I'm not stupid."

"Oh," he said, seemingly disappointed. "No, clearly not. That's a pity. I thought . . ." He trailed off.

"There you go again," I pointed out. "Withholding information, prompting me to think the worst. Well, it's working—I *do* think the worst. I think . . ."

He held up his hands in an obvious placatory gesture.

"All right, all right," he said. "I'll tell you everything. What I know, what I think, and what I'm trying to figure out . . . as much as you like. But it will take time—please try to calm down. As you say, you're not stupid, and I'm sure you can follow the logic of the argument, if you'll just hear me out. Will you let me explain?"

I calmed down. "Go on," I said.

"Good," he said. "The first case to be brought to my attention, as you've probably realized, just by looking at him, was Lysander's. Initially, I came to the Reservation just to consult with his osteopath. It was a complete mystery—completely unprecedented. We didn't know what to think. Then the second, third and fourth cases came in, in quick succession: Helen, Billy and a woman you haven't met, named Cleo. Well, what would you have done?"

"Apart from worry that it was the start of an epidemic?" I paused, in order to damp down the asperity in my voice as much as to give myself time to think, but then added: "I'd look for a connection between the four cases, of course—try to figure out whether they'd come in contact, or when they had been in the same place at the same time."

"That's exactly what I did. I looked as hard as I could for evidence of possible contagion, or some common factor of vulnerability. I couldn't find one. Then the fifth and sixth cases came in. I'd already begun to extrapolate beyond factors relevant to their lives in the Reservation. That seemed perfectly natural to me, because all my contact with osteomorphism, and all my studies, have been Outside. And for the first time, a coincidence came up. Two of the six victims we now knew about had been associated when they were alive. Immediately, we began to look closely at the lives of the other three, to try to identify some connection between them and the two associates. We only found one very slight but possible connection. Then I flipped the question. I wondered whether any of the other individuals in the same association as subjects one and five had gone on to have a Postmortal osteomorphic existence. And one name came up: yours. So I ordered your file for study, even before Dr. Setlow's notification came in, and when it did, within forty-eight hours, I thought that I might be on to something. It seemed like a breakthrough. Two out of six could have been just a coincidence, but three out of seven . . . that definitely looked like a meaningful link. That's why the ambulance man knew your old name and used it. He didn't realize that it was such a touchy issue . . . and to tell the truth, I didn't quite realize it myself, hence my slip. Now, may I ask you a question?"

"Yes."

"Can you, by stretching your memory as far as possible, remember ever having known Lysander Link on the Outside?"

I did as I was asked, with perfect seriousness. I couldn't. "No," I said. "But that's not surprising. The typical amnesia . . ."

"I know as much about that as any Outsider does," he said. "Can you guess which of the other three people you met a few minutes ago is the other person that you and Lysander knew during your previous life?"

I had to admire the ingenuity of that. I couldn't remember, for the life of me, ever having known her before, but I found, as soon as the question was posed, that I *could* guess.

"Jillian," I said.

He nodded his head vehemently. "Right," he confirmed. "You can't remember, but subconsciously, you do know. That's something for Sthenelais to work on—it's promising."

"You're doing it again," I pointed out. "You said you'd tell me everything—as you should have done to begin with."

"Perhaps so," he said. "The principle of informed consent. Well, Lysander Link was, for several years, the first violin in an orchestra with which you—your human self, that is—played regularly as a solo pianist. Jillian Verdame played the oboe in the same orchestra, during the same three-year period.

"My Larva was a concert pianist?" I queried.

"Yes—didn't you know?"

"Actually, no. I knew I'd been a piano player, but I figured it was probably in a bar, or maybe even just a hobby. You said that only one name came up when you checked. Are all the other members of the orchestra still alive, then?"

"Alive or irredeemably dead—most alive. Lysander was the oldest member, and Jillian died in middle age, of pancreatic cancer."

"And what did my Larva die of?" I asked, automatically.

He hesitated, but he had promised. "You committed suicide," he said, "at the age of twenty-five."

That was a bit of a shock. I had never thought of myself as the suicidal type. Anything but, in fact. "How?" I couldn't help asking.

"A narcotic overdose," he said. "You had a serious problem, apparently. Can you remember that?"

"No," I said flatly. I realized, belatedly, that perhaps I hadn't been entirely wise in demanding that he tell me everything he knew. But it wasn't relevant to me, to Peterkin the school piano-player, who liked Melissa . . . a lot. He was a happy person, a loving person. He didn't have a serious drug problem. How could he? He was a skelly. He didn't have any problems at all . . . at last he hadn't had, until Monday morning.

"You think the drugs had something to do with . . . this?" I held up my left wrist, where *this* was still most obvious.

"It's a hypothesis I'm considering seriously," he said. "Jillian Verdame underwent chemotherapy for her cancer; Lysander Link used medication for chronic asthma. Whether or not that had something to do with your vulnerability to the remetamorphic process, I'm interested in the possibility that it might have had something to do with your achievement of Postmortality, and the specific form of your Postmortality. There are mysteries there, as you know."

I did, vaguely, but Larvae tend to be much more interested than skellies, for obvious reasons, in the mystery of why some Larvae are going to continue their careers beyond death, while others aren't, and with the particular form of Postmortality they might achieve. My interest was focused on the disease.

"And the fourth remote coincidence you found was also to do with . . . medication?" I asked.

"This is the twenty-first century," Dr. Charteris reminded me, unnecessarily. "Everybody uses medication." His *everybody*, of course, only included Larvae, but I didn't bother to correct him. "No," he went on, "the slender connection was to do with music. Helen also used to play the piano—not professionally, but quite well."

I kicked myself, metaphorically, for not having thought of that first. Music was a much more plausible connection for skellies. Skellies love dancing. A concert pianist while alive, I was now a pianist at a ballet school. Lysander, a first violin while alive, was now, as he put it, a "fiddler at the Grand Guignol." There were seeds of a pattern there. But . . .

"What about the other three?" I asked. "Billy, Cleo and the one you haven't named."

"Hector. That's where the argument begins to look shaky," he admitted. "Just as everybody takes medication, everybody listens to music, usually with some enthusiasm, including Billy, Hector and Cleo . . . but not in any way that distinguishes them very clearly from other people with similar backgrounds. We're examining their lives carefully, and Sthenelais is using her methods in the attempt to bring relevant memories back to the surface . . . but, in the meantime, the triple coincidence linking you to Lysander and Jillian in question doesn't seem to me be a matter of random chance. It's a new line of inquiry for me, and an intriguing one."

"And how, exactly, might it help to cure the disease?" I asked.

Again, I couldn't interpret his reaction. For the first time in my afterlife I cursed myself for not having paid more attention to Larval TV. Who could have guessed that the ability to read Larval faces would ever be useful?

"If we can understand the aetiology of the phenomenon . . ." he began.

I didn't know what aetiology was, but I did understand the significance of his referring to the disease as a phenomenon.

"That isn't your top priority, is it?" I said, no longer trying to keep the asperity out of my voice, although I couldn't be certain that a Larva could interpret the intonation of a skelly voice any more accurately than a skelly could read a Larval face. "From our point of view, this filthy red stain is a hideous disease in dire need of cure—but from your point of view, it's a cure of sorts itself, for the disease of being a skelly."

"That's not true!" he protested "We really are trying to figure out a way to reverse the process. Wilhelm . . ."

I didn't bother to correct the name. I was too busy remembering what Billy had said about having to think of possible ways to get rid of the stuff himself, and Dr. Charteris merely observing with interest. Lysander's paranoia was becoming more plausible by the minute. It seemed to me that Dr. Charteris was probably sincere, but the fact remained that his primary interest was in studying the "phenomenon," not in stopping it in its tracks. World's foremost expect or not, he wouldn't have been my first choice as the person in charge of our treatment.

"If not you, Dr. Charteris," I suggested to him, "some of your fellow Larvae might think of what's happening to me as *coming back to life*, and even seeing that as a good thing. Who, exactly, are the *we* to whom you keep referring? Larvae, I assume."

"Actually, no," he was quick to retort. "I brought Henry and Pernel with me, but they're just employees, like Adelaide. My chief collaborator—my only collaborator, for the moment, although we might have to bring in more help if more cases turn up—is Sthenelais."

"The psychiatrist? The ghost?" I queried, just to make sure.

"That's correct. We're consulting with Dr. Setlow and other osteopaths, obviously, but if you think about it, there's nothing odd, let alone anything sinister, in the fact that the scientists who are studying the metamorphic processes that produce osteomorphs and other Postmortals are humans working on the Outside, in the morgues . . . with the intellectual assistance and collaboration of the Ghost Faculty."

He was half-right. When I thought about it, I could see that it did make sense that the people most interested in the metamorphic processes that produced skellies and other Ghetto-dwellers would be Larvae who might have some such transition to look forward to, or not . . . but the assertion that there was nothing sinister about it, even without figuring in the involvement of the Ghost Faculty, was a different matter. I could see that I was going to have to do a lot more thinking about it.

For the time being, I returned to what seemed to me to be the essential point. "But it *is* a disease," I insisted. "And the number one priority has to be finding a treatment for it. You can look at your . . . aetiology later."

"It's not as simple as that, Peterkin," he told me. "I can understand how distressing this is for you, but in order to be able to cope with this phenomenon is future, given that it probably isn't going to go away, even if we can find a treatment for the seven current patients, then we really do need to understand it fully. And although you're insistent on calling it a disease, there are other perspectives—one, in particular, that might require serious consideration . . ."

He stopped, but this time it wasn't just his reflexive tendency to hold back information. This time, he was actually challenging me. Unfortunately, I hadn't the slightest idea what he might be getting at it.

"Go on," I said, after a brief pause.

"Have you ever heard of the zombie evolution?" he asked.

"No," I said, quite unable to see what zombies had to do with anything. "So far as I know, they don't evolve, they just decay. Rotten from the moment their post-mortality arises, they just keep rotting until they turn to slime. No hope yet of a cure, it's said—but I wouldn't know how hard your colleagues who specialize in zombies are working on it, or studying its *aetiology*." That had just become my favorite dirty word, even though I still wasn't certain of its meaning. I am now, obviously: it means the analysis of causation.

"You're thinking along the wrong lines," he told me. "I don't know how much you know about Postmortal history, but you must be very keenly aware of the fact that osteomorphs are very different in kind from vampires, and from lycanthropes, and probably have good grounds for thinking themselves unfortunate to have been stigmatized in the same way and banished to the same Reservation."

"And how," I said. "It's not difficult to see why Larvae spent centuries trying to exterminate vamps and lykes, and succeeded at one time, to the point of having them considered legendary beings—but skellies never drank anyone's blood, or ripped anyone apart, even at the full moon. I suppose we might have accidentally caused a few oversensitive Larvae to die of fright, way back when, but not nearly as many as ghosts did."

"Precisely. The fact that osteomorphs were quarantined, along with vampires and theriomorphs, was a matter of lumping together everything that humans were afraid of, no matter how unreasonably. And initially, zombies were in the same category as skellies and ghosts. They were stupid, docile and essentially harmless, used extensively as slaves, albeit not very efficient ones. And then something changed, not very long ago: the zombie evolution."

"You mean that they developed a penchant for eating brains."

"Indeed. The whole species, over a relatively brief timespan, stopped being harmless, docile and almost mindless, and became dangerous, recalcitrant and, if not exactly intelligent, a good deal more articulate and cunning than they'd been before. They're still rather slow, but they're certainly dangerous enough to warrant locking away in the Ghetto, far too dangerous to carry on doing the traditional slave labor to which they'd once been assigned, in societies that had found methods of stimulating transitions of that specific sort."

Enlightenment began to dawn. "So you think that this," I said, holding up my wrist again, "might not be a disease at all, or even a kind of retrogression. You think it might be a skelly *evolution*?"

"I think it's conceivable . . . and that it might be a more fruitful way of thinking about the issue than either of the simpler perspectives."

"Well, I still want a cure," I said, firmly. "I don't want to evolve . . . certainly not into anything squishy."

"I can understand that. I won't insult your intelligence by wondering how the lemuroid ancestor of the genus *Homo* might have felt about the prospect of not being a lemur any more, because you know as well as I do that the cases aren't comparable, and why . . ."

That was another challenge; unfortunately, it was another to which I couldn't rise. "Okay," I said, "so I'm not as smart as I thought. Why aren't they comparable?"

He seemed surprised rather than triumphant, so far as I could tell. "Because the evolution of the lemur toward humanity can probably be explained entirely in terms of natural selection. Even the early evolution of vampires and theriomorphs, given the relevant mutations, might also be accommodated, with a little conjectural imagination, to the theory of natural selection. But the zombie evolution certainly can't—and if what is now happening to the skellies, or what might happen if this goes on, really is an evolution of the species, it definitely requires a very different model of evolution."

"Well, obviously," I said, trying to make up lost intellectual ground, or at least to keep up appearances. "Skellies don't have genes, and although we have . . . intimate contact . . . we don't have children. Except . . . hang on, I need to think about this . . . skellies aren't a species, as such, merely the final developmental phase of the human species . . . *one* final developmental phase, out of several alternatives. But humans aren't like insects, where the imago is the breeding phase. Humans are topsy-turvy . . . which is confusing. The real question, in terms of the theory of natural selection, is whether—and if so, why—human larvae are being selected out that can go on to produce one kind of postmortal phase rather than another . . . or, indeed, any at all. It's out of my intellectual reach, I'm afraid."

"You're by no means alone in that," said Dr. Charteris. "I very much fear, on my bad days, that it might remain forever beyond mine. The Ghost Faculty have a theory, but—as you might expect—it's heavily biased toward their idea of themselves and their place in the existential schema, and I have problems with it. So will you, if a ghost ever deigns to explain it to you. But in essence, it comes down to the nature and evolutionary capabilities of virtual flesh. That, really, is the nub of the matter. Naturally, you think of what's happening to you as something afflicting your bones, but it isn't—in effect, it's leaving your bones exactly as they are. What it's doing is subjecting your virtual flesh to some kind of atypical metamorphosis. Exactly what kind, we can't be sure yet, but we certainly can't take it for granted that it's simply replicating the flesh you had before, when you were, as you put it, a Larva."

"I see," I said, slowly, still trying hopelessly to catch up with a train of thought that was now heading away from me at top speed. "So, until we see what happens to Lysander, we won't really have any idea of what's likely to happen to me. And even then, it might not be exactly the same thing?"

"Indeed."

"And although you're happy to go along with Billy's repeated attempts to scour himself clean of what he sees as a horrid pollution, he's actually right in thinking that you don't really want him to succeed?"

"As a physician, I'll certainly congratulate him if he succeeds, and wish him well—but as a scientist, as you say, I'd be exceedingly interested to see what happens to him . . . and to all of you . . . if he fails. I really am on your side, though. I know that there's a popular notion in the Reservation that all scientists are mad, especially the ones in your own university, and perhaps it's true, but I really mean you no harm, and I certainly wouldn't subject any of you to any medical treatment without your informed consent. If this is an experiment, it's Nature's, not mine."

"All right," I said, somewhat distractedly. "I'll believe you, for now. I suppose we'd better get back to the consultation we're supposed to be having. What now?"

"Nothing, for the moment. Tomorrow morning, I'll give you a thorough examination, and take some samples of the metamorphic tissue for microscopic examination and analysis. Over time, I'll monitor the development of your condition as closely as I can, comparing it with the development of the condition of the other six patients— and more, if others turn up, as they probably will. I'll have to call in reinforcements, though, if the total rises any further, and we'll probably need other facilities if the number triples or quadruples. You can foresee the problem of that as well as I can. Fortunately, there won't be a problem in transferring some of you to facilities outside the walls."

"Yes there will," I objected. "I have friends—so have the others, I imagine. When your orderly told me about the restrictions to visits, they already seemed like an undue imposition. There's no way I'm going Outside willingly."

"That is an issue," he agreed, "and I'm sorry about having to restrict visiting times and require appointments to be made, but it's a simple matter of practicality. We can't be absolutely certain, as yet, that the condition isn't contagious. I'd really like you to bear with me on that. You're not a prisoner, and I can't prevent you from leaving or having as much contact with as many other people as you wish, but I'm sure that you don't want to expose people even to tiny unnecessary risks any more than I do."

"Fair enough," I said, "but you'll have to consult us all before you think about moving anyone Outside."

"Of course. And I'd also like your cooperation in another way, if you're willing."

"What way?"

"I'd like to try to recover some of the memories buried in your subconscious, if possible, and I'd like you to help with that, if you can. I'd like to find out more about what you had in common with Lysander and Jillian when you were alive. I know it's a touchy matter, but you must be curious yourself, now that you know what I know."

"Exactly what are we talking about? Hypnosis? Past-life Regression?"

"In a manner of speaking. I think Sthenelais prefers to use the term 'assisted meditation.' She seems to have made some progress with Jillian, and also with Lysander. She'll be particularly interested to work with you."

I didn't bother to ask why his shrink was a ghost. Skellies don't go in for psychiatry, but the Ghost Faculty, being a trifle short in the body department, are very keen on soul science.

"I don't know about that," I said uneasily. "I'm not at all sure that I want to dredge up larval memories."

"It might be important . . . to your understanding as well as mine. Some of the others were equally reluctant, when the idea was first broached, but I think they'll come round, as they get used to the idea."

"I'll see what it involves," I said, reluctantly. "I'm not making any promises, though. I still think there's something very fishy about all this . . ."

"There isn't. And I'd really appreciate your cooperation. If we all work together, methodically, we'll get to the answers a lot sooner than we will if there's nothing but resentment and rebellion in the ranks."

"I suppose you might be right," I conceded, that being as far as I was prepared to go, for the moment.

"There's one more thing, before you go," he said, evidently intent on pushing his luck.

I glanced at the clock on the wall, and was surprised how late it was. "Go on," I said.

"I've asked for a piano, and some other musical instruments. Lysander already has his fiddle. The piano should arrive tomorrow. I'd like you to play for us all."

"Not on my own?"

"Ideally, no. I'd be particularly interested to see you play with Lysander and Jillian, obviously—but the more, the merrier. Perhaps those who can't play can dance."

"That will probably be less difficult than the other," I said. "In fact, if you'd just shown me a piano without saying anything . . ."

"But you wanted to know," he reminded me. "You wanted to know what I know, and what I think. Now you do—all but the abstruse scientific theory, much of which, I have to confess, is empty jargon. We're working in the dark here, Peterkin, and we don't really know whereabouts to grope for the light switch, if there is one."

Or whether we'll be able to stand the glare if we find it, I refrained from adding. Aloud, I said: "Thank you, Doctor. I do feel a little better now, at least with regard to paranoid fantasies I was beginning to form. May I go now?—I'm hoping that my friend might come to visit, and it's nearly five."

"I'll get Adelaide to show you your room," he said. "If you care to make a list of things that you'd like brought from your home, I can get Henry to collect them—or you can ask your friend, if you'd rather. We prefer to keep the visits to the ground floor, but as long as there aren't too many visitors at once, we can probably let you have a private room in which to talk."

I immediately decided to give a list of items to be collected from the apartment to Melissa. The more excuses she had to come back, the better. And I bade Dr. Charteris farewell, for the moment.

9

The best laid plans of mice and skellies fare no better than those of any other kind of men. I was down in one of the small reception rooms on the dot of five, absolutely convinced that Melissa would come. She didn't. What I got instead was Phil.

"I'm truly sorry," he said. "Melissa really wanted to come, and I literally had to beg her. She'll come tomorrow, for sure—but it's important. *Really* important."

"To whom?" I asked, sourly.

"To all of us—skellies, that is, and maybe not just skellies. Is it safe to talk in here?"

"How would I know?" I retorted, my mood not having been improved by his answers to date. "As far as I know, there's only one ghost on the staff, and even if she's into lurking inside the walls of the building, she can't be everywhere at once, but according to the TV dramas, the Larvae have all manner of bugging devices."

His question probably hadn't been serious. He had come to talk and he intended to do so, whether the walls had ears or not.

"I work in the Communications Center, just down the road . . ." he began.

"I know," I said. "Melissa went to see you when I was dropped off here. She seemed to think that you might be able to help, or at least that you might know something about what's going on."

"That's why I'm here—to try to help, and at least to tell you what I've heard. It's just rumor, but . . . well, sometimes rumors have a kernel of truth. You might be in a better position by now than I am to judge whether there's any substance in today's. Are they treating you okay?"

"So far. The first consultation was just chat, but I expect they'll get the needles out tomorrow."

"Good. I'll get to the point." He leaned forward in his chair and lowered his voice in a conspiratorial fashion. "There seems to be a political storm brewing up Outside . . . a wave of panic, if you like."

"Because half a dozen skellies are growing red dirt on their bones?"

"No, of course not—the Larvae don't give a damn about that. About the increase in the Postmortal population."

"I remember you saying something on Saturday about the new Ghettoes they're building in Africa and Australia."

"Yes, they're obviously necessary—but the squabble over financing them has served to bring the broader issue to the forefront of public attention."

"What broader issue?"

"The increasing proportion of Postmortal metamorphoses."

"But it's been increasing gradually for decades. Partly because the Larval population is increasing but mostly because morgue practices have been subject to improvement and refinement since the mid-twentieth century, trying to make sure that no one who might come back gets buried or cremated too soon. That's hardly news. In fact, my impression is that the influx of skellies into the Ghetto has slowed down of late."

My awareness of that sort of issue was very vague, and for the first time in my afterlife, I wondered why. Peter Strangland, suicidal concert pianist, hadn't left me any common knowledge of that kind among the memories that selective amnesia hadn't censored. Presumably, he hadn't paid very much attention to that sort of thing, not having given any serious thought to the question of whether he might have a Postmortal life to come, or, if so, of what sort. Why not? What did Larvae have to think about that was more important than a vital matter like that?

"The recent slowdown is because more recent Postmortals and lycanthropes are being held Outside for longer, in anticipation of the opening of the new Reservation," Phil said. "The figures for metamorphosis are definitely on the up, and sharply, especially because of the internationalization of good morgue practice. Effective facilitation of postmortality is now practically worldwide—with the result that if the current trend continues to follow the recent acceleration, the global community will not only need another so-called Reservation, in addition to the one is Australia, within five years—that's the African one of which the plans are already on the table—but two more within ten.

"Although the rate of increase seemed slow for most of the twentieth century, it's now becoming obvious that it's actually geometric, not linear. Given that, it only takes a few swipes of a calculator's keys to tell today's twenty-year-old Larvae that if the trend continues, even though they won't live long enough to see the day when the Postmortal population will catch up with theirs, their children or grandchildren might. That's the kind of calculation that grabs the kind of headlines that are carefully censored from our news.

"Even that wouldn't have caused a serious panic for decades, if it hadn't been for other rumors—the kind that get censored from everybody's news, but which run riot nowadays on the internet. It's being repeated insistently Outside that a team of bioscientists in California has made a breakthrough that will finally allow the Larvae dramatically to increase the proportion of the dead who achieve postmortality: *second lives for all,* as the old slogan used to have it."

I sat up straighter.

"What kind of second lives?" I asked.

"Ghosts. In fact, the rumor-spreaders claim that the team who've made the breakthrough has been working hand in glove with the Ghost Faculty, the culmination of decades of close collaboration."

"Is that really causing panic among the Larvae?" I said. "I thought they didn't mind the prospect of becoming ghosts? The Larval dramas we get on TV always seem to use plagues of zombies or vampires when they want to invoke apocalyptic threats."

I was racking my brains trying to remember what Larvae thought about that kind of thing, whether from experience in my previous existence or reportage in the current one, but I wasn't coming up with much.

"You might think so," Phil said, "but attitudes have shifted since they found out more about ghosts. Back in the days when they thought there was a Spirit World separated from ours by some kind of dimensional barrier, they found it a lot easier to take comfort from the fact that their dead relatives might be happy, content, and safely out of the way there. Apparently, they don't find what they now know, or think they know, about the reality of the matter quite as reassuring. But that's not the point I'm trying to make. The possibility that Larval panic might give rise to an anti-Postmortal backlash is only one side of the issue. You and I, and everyone in the Ghetto who isn't a ghost, also has to consider what might happen to the other Postmortal species if the rumor is true and every Larva might one day have a reliable means of choosing to becoming a ghost after death."

He'd obviously given that matter some thought, and had taken the trouble to become authentically worried. He looked around the walls of the little reception room nervously. They looked perfectly innocuous, painted a commonplace shade of institutional beige, with abstract impressionist paintings in green and brown or black and white, but as I'd already mentioned to him, everybody knows—or think they know—that the Larvae now have all manner of listening devices at their disposal, and everybody knows, too, that clever ghosts can hide inside walls.

After thirty seconds or so, I said: "I suppose we, the vamps and the zombies would eventually die out." I filed away for later contemplation—as if I didn't have enough other things to think about!—the question of what might happen if theriomorphs were to acquire access to a Postmortality of which they presently seemed incapable.

"Exactly," said Phil. "*Now* do you get it?"

It seemed to me that it wasn't that difficult to get, but I couldn't quite see that it was really worth getting excited about.

"Do we really care?" I asked him.

Virtual eyes are limited in their expression, but they can stare. Phil stared. He was flabbergasted. He couldn't understand how I could say such a thing, in response to his calculatedly melodramatic assertion that the rumor he'd heard filtering in from outside—which was, after all, only a rumor—might spell the eventual doom of the skelly species.

"Think about it, Phil," I said to him. "Okay, it would be sad to see our numbers dwindle, and the last surviving skelly might feel a trifle depressed about his isolation—but think of the alternative that you've just sketched out yourself: a world in which skellies, along with all the other postmortal species, are increasing much faster than the human population. Doubtless new rumors are the freshest, but let's not forget the old ones—like the rumor that when the Larvae built the Reservation for us, they were careful to bury a hydrogen bomb underneath it, which can be detonated by remote control, so they'll always have the option of annihilating us at a stroke . . . just in case. Thus far, they haven't had the motivation—but if your hypothetical calculations are headline news . . . well, if you had a choice between the species dying out slowly, of natural causes, and getting blown to atoms in a nuclear explosion, which would you prefer?"

He was still looking at me as if I were insane, as well as a trifle blurred by my developing ruddy squishiness, and perhaps wondering if the two were connected. His virtual gaze flicked sideways again, and he reminded me of Lysander. The epidemic of paranoia obviously wasn't confined to a few diseased skellies, or even to the Ghetto.

"I'd prefer it," he said between clenched teeth, "if we could come up with a plan that would allow us to survive, individually and as a species. Wouldn't you?"

"Maybe," I said. "But isn't that the least likely of the three apparent options?"

"I don't think so," he said. His teeth were still clenched. I got the impression that I was disappointing him, as if he thought that I was a traitor, not just to skellykind but to him. "You have to remember, Peterkin, that the skellies shouldn't be in here at all. We're not vamps or lykes, let alone zombies. We could integrate perfectly well into Larval society, given the chance."

"The chance," I said, "might be a fine thing. On the other hand . . . well, the words *snowball* and *hell* come to mind."

He seemed genuinely puzzled by my line of argument, as well as disgusted. I couldn't help wondering whether he might be right. Should I, in fact, be striking a different attitude? I couldn't expel from my mind the annoying, but surely irrelevant detail that Peter Strangland had committed suicide. What did that say about him? What might it imply about me?

"What happened to the famous optimist?" Phil asked—or perhaps sneered. Then he sighed. "As it happens, though, I have to agree with you about the snowball in hell's chance of the Larvae ever letting us out. Especially now."

He'd lost me while my mind had been briefly distracted. "Because of what's happening to me and my six fellow metamorphosites?" I queried.

"Are there six? And are you really metamorphosites, and not just plague-victims?"

"At present, there are seven of us," I confirmed. "Tomorrow or next week, who can tell? As for the other question, Dr. Charteris seems to think that we're more likely to be metamorphosites than plague-victims. He's supposed to be the world's foremost expect of osteomorphic physiology, and I'm just a piano player, so who am I to contradict him? Time will tell."

Phil leaned even further forward, although it was obviously an effort, because he couldn't be sure that he wasn't going to catch something if our heads actually bumped, or even if he caught a whiff of my unvirtual breath, which might already be taking on additional substance. "I think it's a bioweapon," he whispered. "I think it's being tested, as a potential means of taking us out."

I resisted the temptation to laugh.

"My friends upstairs have formed the suspicion that they're not actually making any effort to cure us," I said, in a quiet but perfectly normal voice, "and Dr. Charteris hasn't exactly issued a convincing denial of that suspicion—but it's a further step to imagine that the condition has been deliberately induced, and an even further one to think that it's been deliberately induced in order to test a method of wiping us out. Charteris seems to me to be a sincere scientist rather than some kind of evil mastermind."

"I didn't say that it was *his* bioweapon," Phil countered, still whispering. "I don't think it is."

"Whose, then?"

Yet again, he looked around, seemingly unable to help it, even though he had to know full well that it was a futile gesture. "The Ghost Faculty."

"The Ghost Faculty?" I repeated, incredulously. "Why on earth would the Ghost Faculty want to unleash a bioweapon on skellies?"

"For the same reason that they unleashed one on the zombies half a century ago. To make sure that they stay locked up in the Ghetto for good."

That, I have to admit, took me aback.

"You think that the zombie evolution was caused by a bioweapon designed by the Ghost Faculty?" I queried.

"I do—and I'm not the only one. There have been whispers for years. It's practically common knowledge." There was a hint of defensive asperity in his voice.

"Wow," I said. "And I thought Lysander was paranoid."

In my defense, I was really missing Melissa, and I strongly suspected that I would never forgive Phil for having persuaded her to let him take her place—not that I had liked him much to start with. The fact that I resented him being there, instead of someone that was much more important to me—or who might well become more important, if I could just get the chance to make it so—might have been prejudicing me against his ideas. On the other hand, it really did seem like a mind-bogglingly unlikely idea that the Ghost Faculty was testing bioweapons for use against skellies.

"Who's Lysander?" Phil wanted to know.

"The fiddle-player with the Carillon of Skulls—someone that my former self used to know in our other life, allegedly. Not that it matters. Why, exactly, are you giving me all this crap about the Ghost Faculty having deliberately given zombies an appetite for brains, and now planning an even more bizarre covert strike against the skellies?"

"Because you're in an ideal situation to track the test. If I'm wrong, you can tell me I'm wrong, and quote me the evidence. If I'm right . . . well, you're now in a better position than any other skelly in the Ghetto to figure out exactly what the weapon is intended to do, how the Ghosts might be intending to distribute it, and whether there's any way to stop it."

"Oh," I said. "Is *that* all?"

"Unless you can recommend me to one of your new friends who has more guts and intelligence."

Gutswise, Billy sprang to mind, or even Helen. I reserved judgment on the intelligence, but I figured that any of them who might be more intelligent than me—Jillian, for instance—would be even less patient in listening to Phil's nonsense than I was contriving to be.

"Look, Phil," I said, trying to play the game, "I'm not sure you should be telling me all this. You might be putting yourself in danger. Walls have ears, and as well as a thorough physical examination tomorrow, I'm scheduled for a session of hypnotic regression with a ghost hypnotherapist."

Apparently, I was better at playing the game than I thought, because he started so violently that he rattled.

"You're *what!*" he exclaimed.

"Don't worry," I said—although the words *pigs* and *wings* came to mind—"it's just a matter of digging into my past life . . . my larval life, that is. I don't think she'll be asking questions about popular conspiracy theories and who might be spreading them."

His virtual brain was obviously working overtime, and still had a certain gymnastic agility in conclusion-jumping. "They think your condition has something to do with your larval existence?" he decided. "They think it might have started there, not in the Ghetto at all?"

"Dr. Charteris does seem to want to explore that possibility," I confirmed. "The only connection he's so far found between three of his seven current patients is that our Larvae once played in the same orchestra."

"That's crazy," he said. The words *kettle* and *pot* came to mind—and I suddenly wondered why my mind was so full of trivial larval clichés, when it seemed to be so carefully avoiding such seemingly major matters as the fact that my larval self had been a concert pianist who had overdosed on some narcotic. The sheer perversity of the skelly condition had never been so blatantly obvious. I wished that the piano that Dr. Charteris had requisitioned had already arrived; I felt a burning urge to play a jig.

"The whole world is crazy, Phil," I told him. "Sanity is not an option."

It was just a smart remark, but I immediately wondered whether I had ever said anything in my entire afterlife as perceptive or as true. Afterlife, I realized, is essentially absurd. Not quite as absurd as life, perhaps, but almost. None of it makes sense. Except, obviously, music and amour, if they could be reckoned to be sense as well as sensation and sensuality.

Wow, I thought, privately. *That really isn't me: not Peterkin the school piano-player. It's not* Peter Strangland *either. It's not even delirium. Whatever's happening to my virtual flesh, it's not just a matter of stain and vulgar substance. It's affecting my virtual soul.*

At that moment, seemingly very distant—because the walls of the building were solid and substantial—I heard the sound of a violin. The muffled sound was coming from the first floor. The music it was playing was assertive, not plaintive, and I could just about hear, at the very limits of my virtual audition, the rattle of tarsals and metatarsals on parquet.

My foot twitched, wanting to tap. Phil didn't seem to be affected. Some people are less prone to that kind of infection than others.

"I've got to go," I said to Phil.

He glanced at the clock. Technically, we still had another hour and ten minutes, but he didn't object. What he had come to tell me, he had told me, and if he had hoped and expected for a longer and more intense discussion, his hopes had already been dented, if not dashed.

"Okay," he said. "Think about what I've said, though. I'll come back again."

"Not tomorrow," I was swift to say.

He stood up when I did, but I needed to make sure that he understood. "Ask Melissa to come to see me tomorrow, if she can," I said to him. "I'd really like to see her. I'll let you know via her when you can come again, if you insist. And give her this for me, please." I handed him the list I'd made of things I'd like brought from home to make my internment a little more comfortable.

He glanced at the list. I think he thought about making a sarcastic remark, but decided against it. He had a spark of decency in him. He nodded his head. "I'm sorry I took her spot," he said. "She'll probably never forgive me. What do you want me to say to her?"

"Tell her that I'm doing as well as can be expected, that I'm very grateful to her for taking me in hand this afternoon, and that I'd really like to see her tomorrow, if possible."

I escorted him to the main door of the building, and suppressed a pang of envy as he went out into the night.

"Get well soon," he said. He wasn't being sarcastic, or even sincere; it was just something to say.

"I intend to," I said, "if it's at all possible."

10

Upstairs, the dance party was in full swing, if you can call six dancers and a fiddler a dance party. There were six dancers already, because Adelaide was joining in. It was easy enough for me to recognize Cleo, by a process of elimination, as well as the male patient Dr. Charteris had named in passing as Hector; her bones and his bones looked almost as old as Lysander's, although that obviously said nothing about the antiquity of their afterlife. Substancewise, Hector didn't look much worse than me, although Cleo was further along.

Adelaide collected me as the line swung past, and I joined in with alacrity, pounding the parquet with a rare frenzy, eager to expel something of the frustration from my soul. I wasn't the only one, by any means. Helen, in particular, seemed to be hurling herself into it as if it might be the last time she ever danced. As for Lysander's playing . . . well, he had acquired more substance than the rest of us, but he certainly didn't give the impression of a lead violinist in an orchestra accustomed to playing the classics. He wasn't in the line, but he wasn't standing still either: he was throwing himself into his performance with a quasi-demonic fervor.

The name of the Grand Guignol is a silly joke, of course, and its décor even more so. I much preferred the Palais, even though you couldn't put your hand on your ribs and say that it was a haven of decorum and good taste. But never, I felt sure, even when the Carillon of Skulls and the Guignol were playing up to their farcical image, had Lysander ever played there the way he was playing now. There was a savagery to it that I couldn't have matched on a piano, whose carefully boxed strings simply weren't capable of that kind of screeching torment.

We danced for a long time, although I wasn't conscious of the time passing, and I suspect that the others weren't either—even Adelaide. We danced like people trying to dance the devil out of their souls, trying to get away from themselves, to exhaust themselves, to dance themselves into another world, spiritually if not literally. Some of them must have done a great deal more dancing during their afterlives than I'd yet had the opportunity to do, but I felt morally certain that none of them had ever danced like that before.

I couldn't help wondering whether the mysterious Sthenelais was lurking in the wall, watching us. Even skellies don't have virtual sight sufficiently acute to pierce solid matter, so ghosts inside walls are invisible to us as well as any squishy with virtual myopia, but they can see through most kinds of solidity, and out of it. It didn't seem at all unlikely that a Ghost psychiatrist might be observing her patients from hiding . . . or, come to think of it, that she might have been observing them downstairs, in the reception rooms. I didn't really care whether she might have taken offense at what Phil had told me, if she had happened to hear us; I was more interested in the question of what she had made of the dance, if she had seen it. Could a ghost understand the fire and fury we'd put into it? I thought not. Ghosts are only ghosts, after all. They might think they can dance, but they can't, really. They might think that they can read skelly expressions and skelly thoughts, because our faces and brains are virtual, but they can't, really. Bones make a difference, to the face and the brain.

I was in no doubt, even then, that any ghost shrink who thought that she was an expert on skelly psychology was lost in vain delusion. And I began to wonder, even then, whether that delusion may be dangerous, for me, for my fellow patients, and even for skellykind.

When the exhaustion we were seeking eventually set in, I was the one that the nurse came to check on first— simply because I was new, I assume.

"It all seems a bit crazy, I know," she said, "but that's understandable. How are you coping?"

"As well as can be expected," I assured her. "I needed that."

She nodded, and was about to turn away to continue her round, when I said: "Aren't you scared?"

She didn't have to ask what I meant. "A bit," she said. "But I'm a nurse. You have to get used to it. And it really doesn't seem to be contagious, unless . . ."

"Unless it has a long incubation period," I finished for her. "But you've checked, obviously, to see whether the seven of us might all have been in the same place at the same time, two or three weeks ago."

"We've checked for the others," she confirmed. "You'll get the third degree tomorrow, along with the prods and pokes. Not nice, but necessary. You understand, I'm told."

"I wish. But yes, I can see the necessity. Thanks."

The moment she had passed on to go and have a dutiful word with Billy, Jillian materialized at my elbow.

"May I have a word with you, Peterkin?" she asked.

"Yes, of course," I said.

"In private," she added.

"Fine," I said.

She didn't mean out in the corridor. She took me to her bedroom. It was identical to mine, on the opposite side of the same corridor. Mine was number 19; hers was number 14. She offered me the only chair, and sat down on the bed. I didn't suspect for a moment that she might be trying to seduce me, even though my bones were by far the most attractive of the male bones available in the clinic. I didn't need Phil's talent for conclusion-jumping to know where her curiosity was coming from.

"Has Charteris told you why he was half-expecting you?" she asked, getting straight down to business.

"Yes," I said. "But I can't remember anything about my larval self except for a nickname, which is probably an artifice. That's typical, isn't it? It's not something we talk about, but the impression I get . . ."

"It wasn't something I talked about, or thought about, before I came here," she confirmed, "but since Charteris found the connection between Lysander and me—the only connection the poor fellow has been able to find, apparently—and the shrink has started probing, I've been thinking about it and talking about it quite a lot, and not just to Sthenelais and Lysander."

"It's been preying on my mind too," I admitted, "even though it's only been a matter of hours. I needed that dance to put it out temporarily . . . and I gathered that I wasn't the only one. I'm not sure my piano-playing is up to that kind of intensity."

"At least you still play the piano," she said. "When Charteris told me that my Larva had been in an orchestra, playing the oboe, of all things . . . well, it's not something to which I'd ever given any thought, but it's not the larval existence I would have imagined, if I'd imagined any."

"From which I infer that you don't remember anything about Lysander, or me."

"I didn't, to begin with," she said significantly.

"But you do now? The hypnotherapy, or assisted meditation, or whatever, is working?"

"I don't know for sure that it's a memory. The trickery doesn't seem to be working on Lysander, but Charteris deliberately didn't tell Lysander, and only confessed to me why Sthenelais was asking so many strange questions because I'd got half way there by deduction. Lysander's a nice enough fellow but . . . not the sharpest tool in the box. When I told him what Charteris had told me, he scoffed at first, and then just shrugged his shoulders. I didn't get around to mentioning the item about a third member of the orchestra being in the Ghetto."

She was looking at me, with eyes that were already slightly viscous, with a certain anxiety, as if half expecting that I might simply shrug my shoulders too and tell her that I had no interest in remembering anything about my larval phase. I wasn't even tempted. I wanted to know what it was she'd been assisted to remember . . . or to fantasize. I was also curious to know about the specific nature of the assistance she'd received—but first things first.

"I guessed part of it too," I told her, "but that was because Henry carelessly gave me a heavy hint when he collected me, and Charteris had to tell me the rest. I don't know quite what to think, as yet, but I'm certainly not shrugging my shoulders. I'm scared. The fuzz is bad enough, without all the ominous possibilities being hurled at me like machine-gun fire . . . the most ominous one being that Charteris isn't even trying to find a treatment."

"I know the feeling," she assured me. "Look, Peterkin, I can't say for sure that I remember you . . . or anything, for that matter. I might simply be suggestible, easily prompted to invent, but once the idea came into my head, it became haunting. It seems to me that perhaps, now, I do remember . . . a boy."

"Charteris says that my larva died at twenty-five," I said, deliberately leaving it at that.

"He told me that mine died at forty," she said. "He told me that we must have known one another, just as we both knew Lysander. What he didn't tell me was how well our larvae knew one another . . . perhaps because he didn't know any more than he was saying, or perhaps because he's still keeping a few cards up his sleeve. You have a friend who works in the Communication Center, I understand? The visitor you saw before coming up to join the dance?"

"How do you know?" I couldn't help asking.

"Henry checked him in. I asked because I was curious. That doesn't matter. Does he have some access, however limited, to this internet thing that they have on the Outside, where all kinds of information are available?"

"Probably not officially," I said, "but he certainly seems to have access to rumors from Outside. What information do you want him to find, if he can?"

"I'd like to know more about the circumstances surrounding your Larva's death. Newspaper reports . . . and rumors, if any."

"Why?" I asked. Perhaps I should have been surprised, but I figured it had been a long day, and my resources of astonishment were exhausted.

"Because I think my Larva might have been implicated in it."

"You think your Larva might have driven mine to suicide?"

"Possibly. I'm more anxious about the possibility that your Larva's death might not have been suicide."

Again no astonishment; I suddenly began to wonder whether it wasn't so much that my resources were exhausted as the fact that chords were being struck in my unconscious. "You think your Larva might have murdered mine?" I suggested, cautiously.

"No," she said, "the idea I've got into my head, one way or another, is that Lysander's larva might have murdered yours."

"Ah," I said. I tried to put two and two together. "Over you?" I added.

"I'm not saying I remember it," she repeated insistently. "I might just have a vivid imagination."

"Have you told Charteris?"

"No. If it's true, he probably already knows, given that he certainly has access to the internet thing, and if it's not . . . well, I'm reluctant to let him know that I'm the sort of person that's prone to delusions of that sort. I thought, on balance, that I'd rather confide in you first, in case you had any ideas on the subject, or it rang any bells in your memory."

She wasn't telling the whole truth, of course, but I couldn't blame her for that. She was experimenting too. She wanted to discover whether my presence, and my conversation, would start ringing any carillons in her own memory. She was talking to me skelly to skelly, or very nearly, but what she was wondering was whether two skellies coming face to face might awaken echoes of encounters their Larvae might or might not have had in another life. I was wondering too—about her, that is; I wasn't getting anything that resembled the surfacing of a distant memory. I quite liked the idea of my Larva possibly having been murdered by a jealous lover's discarded ex, though—it was much more esthetically satisfying than thinking that the stupid little sod had killed himself because he couldn't cope with life.

"It might be important, if it were true," I said, with careful neutrality. "Maybe it would provide a clue to the reason why we all came back from oblivion . . . and all came back as skellies . . . skellies who are now falling prey to Almighty Chance only knows what."

"The idea had occurred to me," she confirmed. Unlike Lysander, she was one of the sharper tools in our particular box. Which meant that it must also have occurred to her that if she mentioned it to me before my session with the hypnotherapist who was supposed to help me recover some larval memories, she might be providing my vivid imagination with a script ripe for suggestion.

I knew, though, that I had to keep my mind focused on the important matter, and not get distracted, by the disease itself or all the bizarre theoretical possibilities that it was stirring up.

The important thing was Melissa. I could see that even more clearly now than I had before. The past didn't matter, and the present was just an enormous pain in the cervical vertebrae. What did matter, enormously, was the possibility of there being a future, and the possibility of my future containing Melissa. Jillian's problems, and the world's, were irrelevant . . . except in so far as they might put me on the track of a solution to my own.

Does the fact that I thought that make me a monster of egotism? Perhaps. If so, though, it was surely forgivable; I was in love. Yes, it was time to admit it to myself; I was totally in love. *Amor omnia vincit* . . . or, if it doesn't triumph over everything, at least it excuses everything. I didn't know the Latin for "excuses." I wasn't even sure that the Romans had a word for it, as I had a vague idea that they hadn't been a very apologetic sort of people. Triumphant, yes, apologetic, no . . . but the point was, that I was entitled to be selfish, and to put my own objectives before Jillian's, before Phil's, and most certainly before any interests that the Larvae and the Ghost Faculty might have.

I tried to pull my mind back to the matter in hand. I still had to put on a show of caring about Jillian's supposed problems, whether I actually cared or not.

"You raised the possibility," I ventured, "that you'd come up with this idea by way of suggestion, on the part of the Ghost psychotherapist?"

"That's right. But I don't think that the shrink was trying to put that particular idea into my head. She was just trying to provoke *something*, and that's what my imagination came up with."

"What's she like?" I queried.

"Who can tell? Ghosts are essentially mysterious. They take pride in it. She tries to seem sympathetic but . . . well, she's a member of the Ghost Faculty."

I hadn't had very much contact with any Ghosts since my arrival in the Ghetto, but I had a fair idea what she meant. I couldn't have explained exactly why, at the time, but the phrase "Ghost Faculty" had always summoned up various ideas in my mind, just as the phrase "Mad Scientists" did. There wasn't any logical reason why the great ghost intellectuals had to have been hatched from Larvae who had died old, let alone that they had to have been scientists even when they were Larvae, but that was just the image that my mind had attached to them, assisted by the fact that Ghosts are so secretive, in general, that there's very little hard information to facilitate the building of any kind of image. Ghosts are invisible and elusive in more ways than the crudely literal. Skellies, possessed of purified virtual sight, can see them far more clearly than the occasional seers among the vamps, lykes and zombies, but we generally don't bother to look. I had probably been more curious than most, but I couldn't honestly say that I cared.

Even so, it did occur to me that ghosts, in general, might not be sorry to discover that skellies, in general, might be in the process of growing blurry eyes . . . or might be interested in testing a technology that might enable them to blur skelly eyes, just in case they should ever find it necessary, or politic . . . or simply because they didn't like the idea that skellies could see them more clearly than other Postmortals, if they cared to look . . .

But I had a conversation to carry on, so what I actually said to Jillian was: "I'll have to be on my guard tomorrow, I guess, when she starts messing with my mind. I'm glad you warned me, though. You weren't tempted to wait until tomorrow night, to see whether I'd responded to suggestion myself?"

"I thought about it," she admitted, "but I wasn't sure what it would prove if you did come up with the same suspicion. How do you feel about the possibility that your Larva might not have committed suicide?"

"I don't know," I said. "I hadn't even got around to investigating myself seriously to see how I felt about the possibility that he had. It's difficult, in my present state of confusion, for me to know what I feel about anything."

That was a lie, obviously. There was one thing I knew exactly how I felt about: the only thing that mattered.

I think Jillian was about to say that she knew how I felt, but she didn't have time. The door of her room opened abruptly, without anyone having bothered to knock. Lysander came in, and closed it behind him.

"I thought so," he said. Blunt tool or not, it can't have been difficult for him to work it out, even if he hadn't noticed us leaving the common room together. "She's told you, Peterkin, hasn't she . . . what Charteris told her."

"Jillian didn't have to tell me anything," I told him, mildly. "Dr. Charteris told me himself."

"And?" he said.

"And what?"

"Do you remember anything, of course—about your Larva knowing our Larvae?"

"No," I said, simply. "Do you?"

"No," he confirmed, with what sounded like a hint of relief. "Do you think it matters?"

"I don't know," I said. "That's what Jillian and I were talking about. There is a possibility that it might give us a clue as to how or why we've all come down with this disease."

"Charteris seems to be obsessed with that," Lysander agreed. "Personally, I'm with Billy: the point isn't to understand it, but to find an antidote, quickly. Billy's the one who's actually trying to lead the way, trying to come up with new possibilities to try—except that I have a sneaking suspicion that he's not that bright. You two might be better off talking to Billy about possibilities of treatment for which he hasn't yet volunteered than getting bogged down in the Doctor's crazy ideas about things that might have happened to our Larvae in another life."

"You're being a little hard on him, Lysander," Jillian put in. "Billy's showing a lot of enterprise, it seems to me, as well as bravery—and Dr. Charteris is helping him. I'm not sure that I could come up with any ideas that haven't occurred to them already."

"And I'm just a piano-player," I put in. "Even if I were clever, it would take me some time to catch up with the rest of you, having only arrived a few hours ago. I ought to say, though, that you really did a first-class job with the violin just now. I really needed that. I've been to the Grand Guignol, so I've probably heard you play, without knowing that it was you, but I've never heard anyone play with that kind of fire before."

Lysander was almost in a position to blush at the compliment, but not quite—in fact, he looked horrible, and probably looked even more monstrous by Larval standards than skelly standards. "Thanks," he said. "It's more fever than fire, I fear. We're all under stress, as you've doubtless noticed."

"I have," I confirmed, "and I understand exactly what you mean when you say that it's more important to concentrate on the practical than the theoretical, but ever since Dr. Charteris told me that my Larva and yours were acquainted, something's been niggling away at me. May I ask you about it?"

He looked distinctly uncomfortable, but that was hardly surprising, and might have had nothing to do with the question. "What?" he said.

"According to Dr. Charteris," I said, "your Larva was first violin in what he implied was a pretty fancy orchestra, and I was a soloist. Here, we're both . . . how shall I put it . . . ?"

"Slumming?" he suggested, dryly. "Well, even though my bones are a lot older than yours, we've neither of us been in the Ghetto very long. We both had to start at the bottom again, and, let's face it, the opportunities available to a fiddler and a tinkler in Skellytown are a trifle restricted."

"Maybe that's it," I agreed. "But . . . well, I can't help thinking that I'm happy now—or was before this stuff started growing on me—and life seemed to be on the brink of getting even better. If what Charteris tells me about my Larva is true, he doesn't seem to have been happy at all, and doesn't seem to have seen any future at all. I can't help wondering if that's somehow significant."

Lysander looked at me with an utterly unreadable expression, but that was hardly surprising, given his strange physiognomic resources. "Are you asking me whether I was happy here before this thing started wrecking my life?" he queried.

"Actually, I was assuming that you were," I said. "We're skellies, after all. We're a happy breed, on the whole, aren't we? Vamps and lykes are notorious for their distinctive species of angst, and the possibility of zombie happiness seems an utter absurdity, but skellies, by and large, seem more than content with their lot. If what we see on Larval TV is reliable, they're almost as bad as vamps and lykes. I've never thought about it before, obviously, and perhaps now isn't the time, but it's made me wonder whether one of the reasons that some Larvae manage to metamorphose into skellies is because they have a deep-seated urge to find a happier kind of existence than the one they had before . . . which might, I suppose, be part of the reason why our amnesia seems to be much more sweeping than vamp amnesia."

Lysander shrugged his shoulders, with what seemed to me to be a certain contrived deliberation. "Too intellectual for me," he said.

I glanced at Jillian. She too seemed to be wondering whether Lysander might have a hidden agenda, conscious or subconscious, for avoiding the issue.

"You're right, of course," I said. "It's way too deep for me, too. I just can't help the ideas being stirred up. There's another one that would never have occurred to me in a million years if today hadn't been so extraordinary."

Lysander wasn't going to ask, but Jillian couldn't resist the bait. "What's that?" she asked.

"Well," I said, "if skellies are essentially happier than vamps, lykes and Larvae, how do ghosts feel?"

Lysander didn't shrug his shoulders, but maybe they were just tired. "Who can tell?" Jillian replied—but she didn't leave it at that. She went on, thoughtfully: "One of the few things they don't make any secret of is their feeling of utter superiority, and the way they look down on the rest of us—but I'm not sure that *happy* would be their adjective of choice in describing their state of being. I get the impression from my sessions with Sthenelais that they consider our kind of happiness as essentially vulgar—something they've transcended. It might be just an act, of course, and it might be just the supercilious ones, but my vague impression has always been that they care a lot more about being what they think of as clever than what we think of as happy."

"Like I said," opined Lysander, "way too intellectual for me. I'm just a fiddler."

"And I'm just a piano-player," I supplied, "And we're both skellies, so we can't drink to forget. Music is our only option, mind-numbing-wise."

"What's that supposed to mean?" Lysander asked, confirming my suspicion that he had at least a suspicion of what it was supposed to mean and that ideas had popped into his head recently—or had been planted there—that he would rather have kept at bay.

"Nothing," I said. "Look, I've had a really heavy day, and that madcap dance, which was exactly what I needed, has wearied my bones so much that I might actually be able to sleep. Do you two mind if I go to bed?"

"Not at all," said Jillian. "Thank you for talking to me, Peterkin." She didn't add that it had put her mind at rest, or even that it had helped a little, but I thought that her thanks were sincere.

"Sorry, lad, if I've put you out," said Lysander. "Shouldn't have barged in, I suppose . . . but we're all wound up, for obvious reasons."

"Absolutely," I said. "It seems to me that you're all handling it with admirable courage and fortitude. I only hope I can do as well."

And with that, I left, figuring that they might both have questions to ask one another, however warily and however closely they were keeping their cards to their not-so-virtual chests.

11

I had told Jillian and Lysander the truth, or almost. My bones were indeed weary, and I really would have liked to go diagonally across the corridor, open the door to room number 19 and collapse on the bed. The only margin of dishonesty was my expression of the hope that I might be able to fall asleep. In fact, I was pretty certain that I wouldn't be able to sleep, and that my mind would probably be seething for hours while it tried to digest a little bit of the food for thought with which it had been force-fed in the last few hours.

As it turned out, though, the night, if not exactly young, wasn't yet ready to lie down and let me go. I switched on the electric light with which the room was equipped, although it wasn't strictly necessary, but the room wasn't familiar as yet and I figured that my virtual sight could do with the assistance that electric light provided. Then I sat down on the bed, ready to admit a deeply expressive virtual sigh.

I didn't have the time. The ghost didn't bother with the door. She just stepped out of the wall.

This time, I really was astonished. Perhaps I shouldn't have been, given all the ideas that had been planted there, but I was. I rallied, though, with what I thought was admirable alacrity.

"You couldn't wait until tomorrow?" I said, before I'd even taken a good look at her. "Should I be flattered or alarmed?"

"I just wanted to take the opportunity to introduce myself, briefly," she said. "My name is Sthenelais."

"I'd be willing to bet that you didn't inherit that from your Larva," I said. "And if I were in a reckless mood, I'd be willing to bet, too, that you've been following me all day, ever since Dr. Setlow's nurse took off that poultice, lurking inside walls or whatever else was convenient to hide from my virtual sight."

"Why would you think that?" she said, with contrived innocence. She was, after all, a psychiatrist, or posing as one—but I seemed to detect a slight hint of anxiety in her voice, and that was what made me look at her more intently. And it was when I did so, and tried to focus my virtual vision in such a way as to make maximum use of its acuity, that my recently practiced ability for conclusion-jumping really came into its own.

I recognized her. And suddenly, all the paranoid ideas came together, and added up to something *truly* horrible.

Looking back, I now realize that that moment of recognition, as well as unleashing a torrent of terrible thoughts, was something rather remarkable. It didn't seem so at the time; I looked at her; I recognized her, and I never had an instant's doubt that I might be wrong. The fact that I recognized her, however, was obviously utterly unexpected to Sthenelais, having never entered her head as a possibility, and it might surprise a great many of my readers, including a few skellies, who, like me, are perfectly capable of seeing virtual flesh with the aid of their virtual eyes—unlike Larvae, lycanthropes and the other kinds of Postmortals, whose virtual sight, such as it is, is inevitably confused by the psychological dominance of their material sight.

Being able to see ghosts clearly and being able to tell them apart by sight are, however, not quite the same thing. To do that, one needs exceptionally sharp virtual sight, and maybe a knack for recognizing virtual faces. Skellies have practice at that, of course, because we see one another's virtual faces all the time, but we can also see one another's bones, if only by means of the fact that they form a boundary of sorts to the limits of virtual vision, and thus have a relative virtual opacity, as well as a certain inherent virtuosity.

Intellectually, of course, ghosts know that skellies, unlike all the other human species, can see them clearly, and are therefore potentially capable of telling them apart, even though the other species can't. Somehow, though, that theoretical possibility doesn't seem to get through to their thought processes. Partly, that's simple vanity, and the fact that they look down on skellies as failed or aborted ghosts, an inherently inferior breed, but it isn't quite as simple as that. Ghosts can tell skellies apart, just as they can tell members of the other species apart, but they tend to do so by looking at the bones rather than the virtual flesh. That might seem odd, given that they can see our virtual flesh as clearly as we can see theirs, but it probably seems quite natural to them to carry over the same observational techniques they use to identify members of other species to the identification of skellies, given its practicality—and given the fact that it's the way that the other species in the Ghetto learn to tell skellies apart, for want of any other.

So, to cut what could be a tediously long explanation short, Sthenelais had become used to distinguishing all her experimental subjects—or patients, if you want to take her lies seriously for the time being—by means of their bones, not their faces. She might even have made the tacit assumption that I distinguished between my fellow skellies in the same way, although, if she'd paused to think about that the way I'm pausing to think about it now, she might have realized how absurd that was, especially with respect to a skelly in love. Yes, Melissa had young and lovely bones, but that wasn't the whole of her attractions, by any means.

One way and another, therefore, Sthenelais hadn't the faintest idea that I had been able to pick her out of the crowd at the Palais on the night when she'd infected me with her experimental disease, no idea that I was capable of noticing that she seemed to be looking at me—and therefore looking at her with puzzled suspicion—and no idea that, because of that inspection, I'd be able to recognize her when I saw her again.

But I could, and I did. And that changed everything, in terms of my readiness to believe Phil's paranoid fantasy. Suddenly, I remembered that even Larvae are fond of saying that just because you're paranoid, it doesn't mean the bastards aren't out to get you.

Perhaps the sensible thing would have been to keep quiet and play it cool, but there was no possibility of that in the circumstances. I exploded.

"You bitch!" I said, with heartfelt wrath. "*You* did this! *You* did this to me, didn't you?"

She was genuinely astonished—and the fact that I'd leapt so immediately and so unexpectedly to that correct conclusion was sufficient even to throw a ghost completely off her guard, and expose her. Ghosts are difficult to read, even for skellies who can tell them apart, but some reactions are simply too obvious to miss.

"What do you mean?" she contrived to say, but in a seriously discomfited fashion that made it blatantly obvious that she knew exactly what I meant, and that the accusation had hit the mark.

My mind was racing, and my memory was sharp—understandably, because what it was remembering was one of the most emotionally intense moments of my afterlife.

"It was when I put my hand on the wall," I said. "When I was talking to Melissa between dances. I thought it had just been my imagination that you were watching me when I spotted you floating over the crowd, and did a double take, but it wasn't. You'd moved closer, inside the bloody wall—and that's when you infected me with your bloody disease. Phil's right—it really is a bioweapon. You really are testing a means of exterminating the skellies!"

"No, no!" she protested, much as Dr. Charteris had earlier, when I'd made a similar suggestion to him. "You don't understand! It's not what you think! You shouldn't think . . . you mustn't think . . ."

"Well, I do," I snapped at her, furiously. "And I'm not the only one! And when I tell the others . . ."

Perhaps that was a stupid thing to say as well, because if I had been entirely right, and not just half-right, I might have had to fear immediate and lethal reprisals. Fortunately, that isn't the way the Ghost Faculty operates.

"Calm down, Peterkin," she said, in what was presumably supposed to be a placatory tone. "Calm down, and I'll explain . . . and when I have, you'll see that there really isn't any need to get excited . . . and that even if you were right, which you aren't, it would still be far better for everyone, including you, if you work with me rather than against me."

I seriously doubted that. For one thing, I didn't believe for a moment that she was going to tell me everything she could, or that anything she was going to tell me was likely to be true—but even if she did, and it was, I was absolutely certain that it wouldn't be in my best interests to work with her and not against her. I was already calm enough, though, not to blurt that out.

"Go on, then," I said, in a markedly more hostile tone than I'd used in order to issue the same challenge to Dr. Charteris.

"Yes," she said, "you're right about one thing, but only one. I was at the Palais de Danse Macabre on Saturday, although how you spotted me . . . well, anyway, I was there, and I can see how that led you, just now, to form the suspicion that I might have . . . done something that you resent . . . although you really don't have any rational grounds for that suspicion. The important thing to establish, between the two of us, though, is that this . . . phenomenon . . . is certainly *not* a weapon, and the Faculty has absolutely no hostile intentions toward osteomorphs. I came to the Palais to take a look at you because of what Dr. Charteris and I had worked out about the connection between your Larva, and those of two of the other . . . residents. My purpose in being here is purely scientific, and we see this . . . venture . . .

purely as a valuable opportunity to study a new kind of metamorphic process."

"To which you subjected me without my informed consent—or anyone's," I pointed out.

"If it had been, in fact, deliberately induced, that would be true," she said, remaining sternly determined not to make any admission of guilt, even though she must have known that it wasn't going to make any difference and that the idea was firmly fixed in my mind for good.

"I *know* you did it," I said, flatly, looking her straight in the virtual eyes. I suppose I didn't, really, but even the possibility was enough to make me angrier than I'd ever been in my afterlife before.

I expected her to try to talk me out of it, but she didn't. Instead, she changed argumentative tack, and said: "Well, it really doesn't matter, does it, Peterkin? However you contracted the condition, the fact is that you have it, and it's very much in your interests to work with Dr. Charteris and myself in trying to . . . solve the enigma. You have nothing to gain, and everything to lose, by trying to oppose us. That's not a threat—just an analysis of the logic of the situation."

In fact, of course, it was a naked threat—naked enough to make me realize that I really didn't have any substantial resources with which to fight it.

"Do you really expect me to keep quiet?" I asked her, by way of stalling.

She had collected herself fully by now. "Yes, certainly," she said. "In fact, there's every reason why you should. It might be very useful to us, in fact, to have a collaborator within the experimental sample, given the fact that the other members of the sample are . . . restive. You could be an invaluable calming influence, if you're prepared to see sense."

"You really are Mad Scientist, aren't you?" I said. "Whatever threats you're aiming at me, you'd have to be crazy to think that I'd actually help you in this murderous enterprise."

"I have no intention of making any threats," she lied, "and it's *not* a murderous enterprise. Our objectives are entirely benign, and it really is in your interests to help us. We can make it worth your while."

My mind was still racing. Mostly it was telling me that I was over a barrel, and didn't have a single card to play—but then, suddenly, I realized that I did have one, although I didn't know whether it was capable of taking a trick.

"You were watching me at the Palais," I said, still working it out even as I voiced the train of thought. "You were there, as you say, because of Charteris' hypothetical prediction. That's why you wanted to infect me. But he doesn't know that you're manipulating him, does he? He doesn't know that you're leading him by the nose—and it won't matter how ardently you deny it, if I tell him that you're playing him for a mug."

She was still calm and collected; she hadn't been on her guard before, and I'd taken her completely by surprise. It wasn't going to happen again.

"I'd really rather you didn't make that suggestion to him," she said, serenely, "even though it's utterly absurd. In fact, I need to ask you, rather urgently, not to do it. I repeat, it really is in your best interests to work with me rather than against me."

"There are a million things I'd like to know," I said, "but I'll settle for one before I listen to whatever else you have to say. *Have you got an antidote?*"

She hesitated, long enough for me to suggest that the simple answer was yes, but she stuck to her tattered game plan: "We're confident that we can find one . . . eventually . . . as long as everyone cooperates with our investigation."

There was the threat again.

"And that's why it's in my interest to help you?"

"One reason. There are others. For instance, I can offer you lucrative employment—far more lucrative than playing piano and teaching ballet in a school."

I thought that it said something about her state of mind that crude bribery was what she placed at the head of the queue, but I figured that I ought to be glad of it. I didn't really fancy my chances of staying ahead of her in any sophisticated game of wits, given that she was presumably a member of the Ghost Faculty's Inner Circle, but, since she seemed to be willing to negotiate, I felt that I had to try.

"*You* singular?" I queried, to gain time. "You said *we* a minute ago."

"If we were to make a formal employment contract," she said, "you'd be working for the Ghost Faculty. In practical terms, you'd be working for my team, and in matters of everyday detail, I would be the one giving you direction."

I made myself more comfortable on the bed, figuring that the discussion might last some time. I was still tired, but I thought that my chances of getting any sleep even if she went away, had now diminished from not much to zero. On the other hand, I knew that I wasn't at my best, and I decided that I had to be exceedingly careful now that the contest had turned seriously nasty. I propped myself up against the wall. I didn't invite her to sit down. Ghosts don't sit, unless they're posing. I put on a show of thinking about her proposition, although I'd already made up my mind what my negotiating position ought to be.

Eventually, I said: "No, I don't want to work for you."

I was prepared to assume that she'd be surprised by that, although I didn't expect any astonishment to show. All she actually said was: "That's . . . disappointing. Would you mind telling me why not?"

"I believe you when you say you can find an antidote," I said, still thinking aloud, "and I strongly suspect that you already have one. What I'm wondering, though, is why you're doing this. On due reflection, I'm prepared to believe, for the moment, that you aren't testing a bio-weapon in case the Ghost Faculty ever gets the urge to wipe our the skelly population, that what you're actually attempting is a genuine exploration of some hitherto-undetected property of virtual flesh, and that you don't intend anyone to come to permanent harm."

I couldn't tell whether she seemed relieved that I'd accepted that part of her story, even though I was watching every feature of her ugly virtual face. At least, it looked ugly to me, but not being a ghost, I couldn't be absolutely sure what the males of her own species might think. She didn't look to me as if her Larva had died young, and a long afterlife probably hadn't done her any favors pulchritude-wise.

"In that case . . ." she began

I raised a bony arm to cut her off. "I haven't finished. Obviously, you have me over a barrel, and could easily blackmail me into doing what you want by threatening to withhold the cure that you probably already have up your sleeve, presumably unknown to Charteris, but the fact that you're asking me nicely implies that you want more than a pawn that you can push around. That's simply not a way of life I want to adopt, though. I don't want to be involved in the Ghost Faculty's murky machinations, even if it's at a rank slightly above that of sacrificial pawn. I'm just a piano-player. If you want my cooperation in the present matter, crude bribery isn't going to cut it. You're going to have to give me some indication of what I'd be cooperating with, and a serious reason as to why it's in my interests to do it."

"I see," she said, sounding neither astonished nor disappointed, although I suspected that she was both. "I suppose that could be called courageous, given your awareness that I have your fate and your future in my hands. I'm intrigued, though, that you're apparently prepared to put some trust in our benevolence, given that your friend Phil's attitude seems more typical of most of the Ghetto's residents." She'd relaxed now, and had settled fully into playing a wilier game. Perhaps she was even preparing to enjoy it.

"Thanks for the compliment," I countered, "but I'm not actually that brave, just hopeful. If even half the rumors that run around about the Ghost Faculty are true, it seems to me that wiping out skellies would be child's play, if you actually wanted to do it, so I'm prepared to assume that you don't. I'm prepared to assume, too, that you have a specific reason for trying out this new procedure you have for transforming virtual flesh, beyond simple intellectual curiosity—that you want the experiment to work, and that you'll make every effort to look after your test subjects. Where I'm being optimistic, obviously, is in making the further assumption that you'll also want to check that the process is reversible, and that you'll be just as interested in turning us back into skellies when the experiment reaches its half way point as we'll be in getting back to normal. Even if you do have that intention, though, what really worries me, a great deal, is how long it might take."

"Because of Melissa," she said. I couldn't detect any hint of smugness in her tone, but that didn't mean that there wasn't any.

I had to grit my teeth. She'd probably been watching me all day, though, with an eager clinical eye, and perhaps for longer than that. In any case, she'd seen me at the Palais when she'd slipped me the poison. Ghosts aren't telepathic, but they have good eyes, and the members of the Ghost Faculty are supposed to be genius level intellectually. She'd seen enough of my conduct to deduce that I was hooked, and that the thought of Melissa giving up on me while I was in the program was a serious worry.

"Well it's not because I'll worry about my pupils missing their ballet lessons," was what I elected to retort.

"I can't offer you any guarantees, obviously," Sthenelais said, "but she does seem to be quite fond of you, and your friend Phil seems more interested in Melissa's friend Salome, so I think your chances are good. Of course, they'd be that much better if you were working for me." She was speaking rather lightly. It might have been mere artifice, but I didn't think so. Obviously, she knew that Melissa's name was a bargaining chip, because that was why she'd thrown it on to the table, but I was prepared to bet that she didn't realize what a high-value chip it was. If rumor can be trusted, ghosts don't rate amour very highly on the existential scale of important matters. They have the virtual equipment, it's said, but not the emotional intensity. I was prepared to guess that Sthenelais thought amour was trivial by comparison with an offer of financial reward. Even geniuses can be stupid.

"I'm still not seeing a real incentive," I told her, trying hard to match the lightness of her tone. "May I ask a few questions?"

"If it will help you to make up your mind," she conceded, warily. "But I won't promise to answer them all."

"That's only to be expected." I didn't add that it was also only to be expected that she would lie through her virtual teeth if she thought it advantageous, but sometimes you can learn a lot from the refusal to answer questions, and even from lies. "Mercifully," I went in, "I think I'm now in a position to guess a few of the answers myself. We can take it for granted, of course, that the Ghost Faculty's ultimate objective is to rule the world, and that this project is one tiny part of your grand plan?"

"I'm not that ambitious," she said. "I'm just a scientist, interested in pushing back the frontiers of knowledge."

"So you're not interested in politics? You're not involved in putting about the rumor on the Outside that a means has been discovered of giving any Larva who wants it a sure-fire way of guaranteeing an afterlife as a ghost? Nor are you doing that as a distraction tactic, prompted by the flare-up of anxiety among the Larvae regarding the expansion of the Postmortal population over the next hundred years or so?"

She could just have said "Of course not," but she didn't. "Can't you believe that such a means exists?" she countered.

"Of course I can," I parried. "In fact, I'm prepared to wonder whether you might have had it for decades, maybe even centuries. I suspect you might have been using it, too—but very selectively."

"And why would we do that?" She was probing, trying to get a more detailed picture of my thinking.

"Oh, come on, Sthenelais," I said, still trying as hard as I could to imply that we were on an equal footing in the verbal competition. "I may be just a piano-player, but I'm not stupid. Because the Faculty wants to rule the world—and because you won't even be able to rule your own kind effectively if you can't control your population rigorously, in terms of both quantity and quality.

"I don't know how long you've been working on it, but logic suggests that your intellectual evolution has pretty much matched the pace of Larval intellectual evolution, so my guess is that you haven't been able to make serious plans for any longer than a couple of centuries. I don't know how long-lived you are by comparison with Larvae, although you're surely not immortal, but whatever the numbers are, any plan your nineteenth-century ancestors made had to be long-term, difficult, multifaceted and underhanded, and it's only gained in complication in the interim.

"One further guess I'm willing to make is that you care a great deal about which Larvae turn into ghosts and which don't. Another is that you have reasons for wanting to preserve the other Postmortal populations—because you think that there are things you might be able to learn from them that will assist you in the calculated manipulations of both squishy and virtual flesh that you need to master, in order to bring your long-term plans to the utopian goal you currently have in mind."

"That's very interesting," Sthenelais observed—meaning that it was interesting that I'd been able and willing to deduce it rather than interesting in itself.

"But what I don't quite understand," I told her, "is why you didn't simply randomize the frame of your current experiment, when it would have been so easy to do. Why include Lysander, Jillian and me, when it would have been so easy for you to obtain seven, or seventy, experimental subjects who had no identifiable connection?"

"Isn't it obvious?" she countered, with what might have been the ghost of a smile.

Actually it wasn't—but I could see some possibilities. "You knew that Charteris would find the connection between Lysander and Jillian," I continued, thinking aloud, "so you knew that he'd form the hypothesis that I might be in line. But why? I can't believe that it was just to lead him down a theoretical blind alley. Unless, of course, it's not a blind alley, but a path to an eventual conclusion you want him to draw, or a line of inquiry that you want him to pursue. When I said that your schemes are multifaceted and underhanded, I wasn't overstating the case, was I?"

"I have to admire your ingenuity," she said, "but there isn't a word of truth in this paranoid fantasy."

I decided to take the inference from that remark that I was probably on the right track.

"The suggestion you fed Jillian is the truth, isn't it?" I guessed. "Whether she's really remembering it or not, it's what happened. Lysander Link really did murder Peter Strangland out of jealousy, disguising it as a suicide?"

"Yes," she said, bluntly.

I thought about the implications of that.

"Does Charteris know that?"

"Of course he does."

She was letting me know, subtly, that Charteris hadn't told me everything, in spite of his promise—that he was playing games just as she was . . . and me too now, I guess.

"And are you responsible for the fact that all three of us were reincarnated as skellies?"

"Absolutely not," she said. "But when the triple coincidence occurred, it did catch our attention, and engage our interest." That was a concession, of sorts.

"And it made you want to engage the interest of the world's foremost expert on osteometamorphosis? Because he hadn't noticed it off his own bat, and you want him to follow it up . . . but you want him to think that it's his own idea."

"What a convoluted mind you have, Peterkin . . . for a piano-player."

Somehow, it seemed more like a compliment than an insult. There was obviously something I was missing, some reason why she was playing the game. Unlikely as it might seem, she really did seem to be interested in me, prepared to tease me rather than simply take off her velvet glove and order me to play ball or else.

"But the experiment can't be just a cover for investigation of that petty mystery," I ventured. "There has to be something bigger at stake, but while you're chasing that, you're really hoping that Charteris might find some clue in the personal histories of Lysander, Jillian and me, and other skellies, to the mystery of why some Larvae metamorphose into skellies rather than, say, vamps?"

"That would be an interesting thing to know," she said, making it sound like an admission. But there had to be something that was still missing; something I hadn't thought of—yet.

In the meantime, I plugged on.

"And you picked us as test subjects because we're extraordinary—because it's sometimes possible to learn more from anomalous cases than typical ones?"

"We're straying from the point," she said, but she didn't sound impatient.

"The answer's still no," I told her, "I don't want to work for you, unless you can give me a better incentive."

"I thought you were already doing that for yourself," she said. "If the answer were, in fact, still no, then I would be disappointed, but I can't believe that it is. Do you really want to go back to playing the piano in the school, when you could put your logic and intuition to work more fruitfully?"

"I'm happy there," I told her.

"You were," she corrected me, "for the time being. But how long could your contentment have lasted, especially if you really can strike up a mutually rewarding relationship with Melissa? You'll want more, for her sake, and for your own. Your ambition has been patient, but it can't lie dormant forever—not now. Look at the way you've thrown yourself so avidly into this mystery. It's been an eye-opener for both of us. I can't claim credit even for predicting it, let alone provoking it, but it's not irrelevant to me . . . to us."

"Your team?"

"The Ghost Faculty."

That seemed to me to be confirmation that the Faculty had had their eye on me for some time. I could only see one likely reason, albeit a bizarre one.

"Are you punishing us?" I said, wonderingly. "Not just Lysander and Jillian, but all of us . . . even me, although I suppose you had to involve me anyway, in order to channel Charteris' speculations into the right funnel? Are you punishing me for getting myself murdered?"

"That's ridiculous," said Sthenelais. "I'm offering you a lucrative job. I won't hold it against you that you don't seem particularly grateful, but you must see that, from our point of view, it's a big favor. It's not the outcome for which we'd once hoped, but still . . ."

Another idea occurred to me, reading between the lines of what she was saying—while still bearing in mind, obviously, that it might all be lies, just bait on a hook. "I wasn't supposed to become a skelly, was I?" I guessed. "You were lining my Larva up in order to make me a ghost . . . before I got myself killed."

She actually seemed pleased. I suddenly had a horrible feeling that I was being led—that, like Charteris, I was being subtly directed toward the conclusion she wanted me to reach, while believing that it was my own idea. She was right—suddenly, I did seem to have a strangely convoluted mind, which I'd somehow never managed to notice before, in the course of my relatively brief afterlife. I realized that I desperately needed time to think about all of this, and try to figure out exactly where my interests did lie. But what I needed most of all was a good night's sleep . . . which didn't seem to be even a remote possibility.

Sthenelais had paused slightly, presumably weighing up exactly how much information she ought to feed me, for the moment, but she was a quick thinker, and someone far more used to making rapid decisions than I was. "You still had a long way to go, Peterkin, believe me," she said, "but yes, you're right, even with the limited means at our disposal, the Faculty had identified your Larva as a candidate. We hoped that you might be able to develop your potential to the level where it might be worth recruiting you, but . . . well, you know what happened. We still hope, though, that you might be useful, that you might still have potential worth developing. And I'm hoping that you really don't need any more incentive than that to join us. As you seem to have accepted, very intelligently, we really are trying to improve the world, difficult though that that is, given Larval . . . mental limitations. It really does require enormous patience as well as ingenious planning. And you can be a part of that, if you want to be—a bit part, admittedly, but a part. How could anyone turn that down?"

"I see," I said, although it would have been more accurate to say that I was completely at sea. "Well, I'll think about it—but I'm not promising you an answer, even when we have our scheduled meeting tomorrow. I really do need time to weigh this up, when I'm not so tired. I do have one more question, though, which might seem irrelevant to you, but it's something that occurred to me . . ."

"The answer's yes," she said, interrupting. She just had to show off. Vanity wouldn't let her allow me to dictate the course of the discussion.

"So what's the question I want to ask?" I said, not quite able to take it on trust that she had guessed correctly.

"The question you asked before you left Jillian's room," she said "Are ghosts happy? And the answer is yes. Jillian was right too, of course, in suggesting that our idea of happiness isn't the same as the average skelly's, but you're not the average skelly. And when she said that we'd rather be wise than happy, she was looking at the matter a trifle crudely, because they're not alternatives, in our way of thinking. Our happiness consists of being wise, and our wisdom in being happy."

"But I'm not a ghost."

"You don't have to be a ghost to adopt that philosophy. The vampire elite do, and even the best of the theriomorphs. You'd have to be a zombie to be incapable of thinking that way . . . and zombies are pretty much incapable of thinking in any other way, alas."

"But you did try, didn't you?" I suggested, figuring that another wild guess couldn't do any harm. "The zombie evolution was a colossal cock-up, but it wasn't malevolence. You really were trying to help, but the plan went awry."

Again, the simple thing to do would simply have been to deny it—but again, she didn't seem displeased by the fact that I'd made the conjecture.

"And how," she said regretfully. "Yes, you're right again, the Faculty did cause the so-called zombie evolution; for once, the rumor mill is spot on in that regard. But yes, we really were trying to help. We were trying to make zombie brains work better, to make them more intelligent. It worked, too . . . but we hadn't anticipated the side effect."

"And you can't actually guarantee, can you," I said, thinking that it might qualify as scoring a point, "that your present experiment won't go horribly wrong too, because of some unanticipated side effect?"

"We're fifty years wiser now," she told me, "and we've been *very* careful in the interim. But no, I can't give you an absolute guarantee. There's no such thing. That's why it's so important to monitor the field trial with the utmost care."

"You could just let well alone. Skellies aren't in need of an evolutionary spurt—certainly not a spurt that involves putting on flesh. We're happy as we are."

"So I'm told. But osteomorphs aren't the only possessors of virtual flesh—they just happen to be one in which metamorphoses of virtual flesh are clearly visible, easy to track and study."

"Ghosts would be just as convenient, then, if not more so. Or is it simply that you consider skellies more akin to experimental animals than your human kin? Is the Ghetto just your laboratory, and the other inmates merely experimental guinea pigs?"

"No, of course not," she said—probably lying again, I thought. "We do consider them our kin, and that's why we want to help them."

"Except that your idea of help might well be different from theirs—from ours?"

"It's in everyone's interest for us to learn as much as possible, as rapidly as possible, about the biology and chemistry of Postmortal metamorphoses. You must be able to see that, Peterkin, and you must realize that it's the most important work that anyone, of whatever species, could be doing. Again, what I'm offering you is a golden opportunity to be a part of it; I really can't understand why you would want to say no."

She really couldn't. "If I were to say yes," I said, "what would you want me to do, exactly?"

She sighed, rather theatrically, and said: "Thank you." She wasn't being presumptuous. She knew I hadn't actually agreed to anything. I hadn't made any commitment at all; but I didn't feel any need to point that out. "I'll tell you tomorrow," she went on. "We'll have at least a full hour to continue this discussion, when we're both less tired. In the meantime, don't do anything reckless. Keep quiet, for now, and we'll see tomorrow whether we can come to a mutually rewarding agreement. For now though, I'm tired. Ghosts need to sleep too, you know."

I did know, and I figured that she had probably had an even busier day than me, so I was almost prepared to believe her. On the other hand, she might just have been stalling . . . but either way, I knew that I was in no condition to continue a game of wits, even with a ghost as close to exhaustion as she might be. Nevertheless, I didn't want her to have the last word, so I was a trifle miffed when she added: "Until tomorrow, Peterkin," and simply stepped through the wall. Ghosts are so theatrical—it's in their nature.

12

The following morning, I was up bright and early. If I'd needed breakfast I would probably have been the first one down by quite a margin, but so far as I knew, only Lysander, Helen and Billy had reached a point where the raw meat on their bones needed metabolic sustenance. Even though I hadn't got any real sleep, I didn't feel too terrible; at least I'd been lying down with my virtual eyes closed, and the torrent of thoughts running through my brain could probably have passed for a dream—or a nightmare—thus fooling my body into thinking it had had an authentic rest. As for my convoluted mind, it had come up with a few more interesting hypotheses that I was eager to try out on Sthenelais, and had firmed up one idea that I was now absolutely determined to try for myself.

Dr. Charteris gathered us all together and gave us a pep talk before the consultation sessions started. It was all bullshit, but I could see how he might think that it was a necessary tactical move, and I even guessed in advance that it would include a judicious leak of information, or even a little embroidery of the truth, calculated to provide a small measure of reassurance to calm the overexcitement of the previous day.

"We have reason to believe that the condition is reversible," he told us. "We don't know exactly how, as yet, but we're fairly certain that it can be done. As osteomorphic physicians, we've only been studying the species scientifically for a hundred years or so, but osteomorphs have a much longer history than that, obviously. Serious scientists haven't recorded anything like it before; it's new to our studies, so there's nothing in the textbooks—the medical textbooks, that is. In history books, though, there's some evidence of previous phenomena. Even reading between the lines, the inference we have to take is that the last time the phenomenon was commonplace was the fourteenth century, before proper record-keeping began. When we dealt with the relevant reportage in medical school, I was initially taught that it was just a legend, symbolic of your servitude to the Larval. It seems to be five hundred years since the last case was even *rumored*. But if there's any truth in the legend, and any truth in the rumor, it's not a permanent condition. It passes. So you mustn't lose hope, or become excessively anxious. In terms of seeking a specific treatment, however, if we're not breaking new ground here, we're starting from scratch."

"You can say that again," Billy said, fingering his bare arm.

"We'll lick it, given time," the osteopath said, firmly. "If your ancestors could get rid of it, so can you."

"Except that they forgot to leave us the recipe," Lysander retorted. "In the meantime, we'll soon be able to lick things *literally*. Will we be still be able to talk normally, do you think, when we have real tongues? Or will we have to go back to doing even *that* the hard way?"

"You're scaring poor Peterkin again, Lysander," Jillian said, reprovingly. "Dr. Setlow didn't send him here to be frightened half to life. We ought to be backing Dr Charteris up, not challenging what he's telling us."

"No," Lysander muttered, "Setlow and his cronies didn't bring any of us here to frighten us half to life. They brought us here to hide us away, to keep us out of sight and out of mind."

"You don't have to stay if you don't want to, Lysander," Dr. Charteris said, sharply. "You can go home any time you like. You're a free skelly—just like Dr. Setlow, or young Peterkin here. Do you want people to see you?"

Hector, who had only arrived in the clinic a few days ahead of me, had obviously been doing some hard thinking since he'd arrived. "Have you considered the possibility that you might need some additional consultants?" he asked Charteris. "I mean, the problem is flesh, not bone or mind, so maybe we need doctors who are used to dealing with flesh, rather than osteopaths and psychiatrists."

"That's a fair point," said Charteris, "and we already have histologists and physiologists looking at all the tissue samples we've so far been able to collect. The more we can obtain, the more tests we'll be able to carry out, and the more consultants we'll be able to call in. I know it's difficult to be patient, but just keep focusing on the idea that you *will* get well, eventually, and in the meantime, take what comfort you can from the knowledge that you're making a contribution to the advancement of science and medicine."

"But Larval consultants are highly likely to look at the question backwards," Helen objected. "They'll take it for granted that flesh is a good thing, something healthy. They're likely to assume that we're getting *better*—that this is some kind of *miracle cure* for the skeletal condition. They probably can't understand that, as far as we're concerned, the whole point is to find a way to *stop* it."

"No, no," said Dr. Charteris, "that's not the way any of them thinks. They're scientists; they look at everything objectively. They understand that the power to destroy is just as important as the power to create. I'm sending samples to a number of oncologists, whose invariable priority is to attack tumors, and who will look at the samples in that context. Cancer treatments have made great progress in recent years—it's entirely possible that one of them will be able to suggest a treatment capable of obliterating the undesirable cells."

That drew nods and murmurs of approval from the others. That was an argument that they understood, and liked.

"But I'm already trying radiation therapy," Billy pointed out, "and surgical removal. So far, the stuff doesn't shrink, and if you cut it away, it just grows back."

"There are still many possibilities we haven't tried, in terms of chemical agents, and there's a huge range of chemotherapies available nowadays for use in tumor destruction," Dr. Charteris countered. "As soon as something has shown promise *in vitro*, you can be sure I'll call for volunteers—but only if I'm sure that it's safe."

"Count me in," said Billy. "I'm game."

"Thank you, Billy," said the Doctor, who was already heading for the door, without asking for questions or further comment.

"I'm desperate," Billy added, turning to scan the rest of us with a panning gaze. It wasn't difficult to believe him; he really was in a shocking state.

Jillian leaned toward me and said: "What do you think, Peterkin? Is he just trying to jolly us along, or is he really optimistic?"

"He's right that there are lots of chemotherapies that haven't been tried yet," I said, judiciously, "and the more samples he collects and farms out, the more chance there is of hitting on something that looks promising. There are seven of us now . . . and who knows how many more cases might turn up in the next few days? It's easy to understand that Billy's nerves are wearing a bit thin, and Lysander's, but you and I, and Hector, already have an advantage in being behind them in the queue. There's every reason for us to cut Dr. Charteris a little slack, and every reason to do what we can to keep one another's spirits up."

I honestly didn't feel like a traitor. I was doing exactly what Sthenelais had asked me to do—or ordered me to do, as she probably saw it—but on that particular issue, I thought it really was in our best interests. In any case, I needed time to put my own plan into action.

"That seems like good advice to me, Peterkin," Cleo put in, having been eavesdropping. "A positive outlook always helps. You're getting your piano today, aren't you? That'll help cheer us all up, I hope."

"Will it?" Jillian queried, looking at me as if she found it hard to believe.

"I hope so," I said, loyally. "I'm not looking forward to all the probing this morning, but if my girlfriend comes to see me this afternoon, that will be a big boost to my morale—and I'm seeing the psychiatrist this afternoon, too. I've heard that she's supposed to be very good."

"Where did you hear that?" asked Jillian, a trifle waspishly, possibly because I'd mentioned the word "girlfriend," or possibly just because I certainly hadn't heard anything good about Sthenelais from her.

"Not from me," Hector put in. "Ghosts think they know everything, but what do they know about skellies? There are tens of thousands of us in the Ghetto, for Almighty Chance's sake—there must be at least one shrink among us."

"Actually," I said, "I don't think there is. Only the Ghosts have had the opportunity and the motivation to make a general study of minds, taking in all the human species. They *are* the real experts."

"Charteris has got to you," opined Jillian, incorrectly. Nobody had got to me, whatever they might think—but for the time being, I was content to lie low, do what I'd been asked to do, and bide my time.

"He is the man with the expertise," I said, meekly. "So is the psychiatrist. We need to trust them. There are no absolute guarantees, but if anyone can help us, they're the most likely people to do it."

Cleo seemed glad of the encouragement, and Hector nodded, as if he were prepared to be convinced, for the time being, but Jillian drew me into a corner and lowered her voice. "Have you thought any more about what I told you yesterday?" she asked.

"Yes," I said. "I can't say that I've actually remembered anything, but I have a kind of metaphorical gut feeling that you might be right. Perhaps it was suggestion, but even if it was, that doesn't mean that it's wrong. On the other hand, this is another life now; what our Larvae may have been and done isn't really relevant to us. It might be relevant to Dr. Charteris, though, if he can figure out the cause behind the coincidence of our being here."

"You and I aren't the only ones with metaphorical gut feelings," Jillian said. "You saw Lysander last night. If that wasn't a man with a twinge of guilt, I don't know what is. So when you say that this is another life, you're right . . . but maybe not entirely. It can't be just coincidence, can it, that our Larvae died so soon after yours, and that we all ended up in the Ghetto?"

"You think you might have followed me?" I queried.

"Who can tell?"

"And that Lysander followed you?"

"The idea of obsession lasting beyond death isn't exactly new," she pointed out. "it's part of the standard legendry of ghosts."

She had a point. "But we're an exotic anomaly," I pointed out. "It's not a pattern."

"We don't know that," she said. She was right—but I suspected that Dr. Charteris and Sthenelais did know, or were at least in the process of finding out.

I had to go down for my consultation then, and pay my dues in samples of bloody tissue. It wasn't free from pain, by any means, but the experience was mostly just tedious. Dr. Charteris did let me take a peek down his microscope, and he tried to explain what it was that I was supposed to be looking at, but there were too many words in his explanation that I'd never heard before. I had to ask him if I could borrow a couple of introductory textbooks to anatomy and physiology. He seemed flattered by my interest. He didn't know that the Ghost Faculty was in the process of trying to recruit me as a secret agent, and that if they managed to bully me or cajole me into being one, I'd undoubtedly be ordered to jolly him along as well as everyone else, and do my bit to keep everything moving in accordance with the Ghost Faulty plan.

At two o'clock, I was already downstairs, waiting for my appointed visitor, and swearing to myself that if Phil turned up again, I would strangle him. Fortunately it was Melissa. She was carrying a valise containing the stuff on the list I'd asked Phil to give her. I whisked her away to one of the small reception rooms, and told her how much I'd been looking forward to seeing her.

"I'm truly sorry about yesterday," she said. "I wanted to come, but Phil was so insistent, and Salome supported him. I was outnumbered. I'm sorry if I'm weak, but I didn't really have any grounds to insist."

"Not at all," I told her. "You're just polite, and kind. There's absolutely no reason to apologize for your virtues. You're certainly not weak—I saw that yesterday. I'll be eternally grateful to you."

If skellies could blush, she would have done. She lowered her eye sockets modestly. I'd never seen her look so beautiful. I almost told her so, but thought it might be laying it on a bit too thick.

"Have you seen much of Lysander, the fiddler from the Carillon of Skulls?" she asked. "Phil says that he's here."

"Yes, he is," I said. "He's suffering, poor fellow, but he's a useful man to have. He played the violin for us last night. By tonight, I should have a piano, although I'm not sure that my wrist is up to playing it properly as yet. I'll try."

"What are the other patients like?"

"A mixed bunch, but pleasant enough, on the whole. There's a guy called Billy who's avid to try out every possible treatment—quite a hero, in his way."

"Are there many women?"

"Three. All much older bones than mine, although one of them hasn't been in the Ghetto as long—neither has Lysander, come to that, although his bones are much older. There's no one as attractive as you, obviously."

It had never occurred to me before to wonder how or why Melissa's Larva had died so young, but the idea insinuated itself into my thoughts now—as it did for Salome. I told myself sternly that it was as unhealthy as it was irrelevant, but my mind was no longer possessed of the kind of serenity that had been its essential character three days before.

"You don't have any idea, though, how long you'll be in here?" she asked, trying to put it delicately but not really succeeding.

"I'm afraid not," I said. "I'm trying to be optimistic, and so is Dr. Charteris, but I have no way of guessing how long it might take." I figured, of course, that Sthenelais, at least, had a very good idea how long it was going to take, but I certainly wasn't expecting her to explain her timetable to me in detail, and if the idea I'd come up with mid-nightmare actually worked, then her timetable might become irrelevant anyway. In the meantime, I had to handle Melissa delicately too, and not just because the walls surrounding us might have ears.

"You'll lose your job, though, won't you?" she said, anxiously. "They'll have to replace you at the school, even if you're only in here for a couple of weeks."

"Presumably—but it isn't much of a job, when all is said and done. I'm sure I can do better, when I get out. That's not a worry."

That wasn't very well put either, since the phrasing implied that although that particular issue wasn't a worry, something else was. What I had in mind, obviously, was the worry that she might not wait for me, and might take up with someone else in my absence, but I could hardly voice that concern. It would have been presuming too much.

"I can't come to see you every afternoon," she told me. "I can't get the time off work. I can come in the evenings, though." She hesitated, and said: "Salome might be able to come instead. She says that she'll be happy to." She gave the impression that she wasn't at all enthusiastic about that proposal.

"That's not necessary," I assured her. "I'm very grateful to you, though. I'm really going to miss next Saturday evening at the Palais."

"Me too," she said, and added: "I don't want to go, if you're in here. I'll come to see you instead." I didn't tell her that that wasn't necessary. There are limits to heroism—and even if my plan worked, I didn't think I'd be out by Saturday.

The conversation proceeded in a remarkably anodyne fashion. It didn't matter. The important thing was simply being together. But as the time wore on, I became increasingly aware of the fact that a drab reception room in an improvised clinic was not a suitable incubator for the kind of relationship that I hoped to build, and I realized that if I was going to be imprisoned for any length of time, the confinement would increase the probability drastically that it would wither and die. While we still had the best part of half an hour to go, I told Melissa that I really needed to get some fresh air, and suggested that we take a stroll around the courtyard.

"Can you do that?" she asked.

"I'm not a prisoner," I told her. "I can do anything I want. The rules about visiting are for their convenience, not mine. I'm beginning to sense the meaning of the term stir-crazy. Humor me, please."

She didn't need persuading. Outside, where the sky was bright and the temperature not too oppressive, I did, indeed, start to walk round the courtyard, and tried to make it look as if pausing in the middle to chat was simply a matter of chance.

It wasn't. I wanted to make sure that we were as far away from the walls as possible.

"I'm truly sorry about all this, Melissa," I told her, in a low voice. "I'm caught up in something here that's more complicated than it seems. I don't suppose it can do any good, but if you can get a message to Phil somewhere in the open, like this, where nobody can be lurking in a nearby wall, tell him that his conspiracy theories are partly right, but much subtler than he thinks. This really is a Ghost Faculty experiment, not an accident of nature, but he needs to think a lot harder about what the Faculty's long-range plans are. It'll probably take someone a lot smarter than me or him to figure it out, but the Faculty can't have a monopoly on intelligence, and I suspect that there are divisions within the establishment. My horizons are narrower than that: I just want to get out of here, and back to normal, and I've had an idea that just might work. It's risky, but Billy would try it like a shot, if I told him. Maybe I should, but it would be cowardly to let him take the chance alone—it's my idea, I ought at least to share the risk."

Melissa looked frightened. "I don't want you to take any risks, Peterkin," she told me. "Couldn't you just tell the doctor?"

"The doctor's a dupe, and the real experimenter wants me to help her lead him by the nose. Maybe I should bring him out here, or even just tell him what I know in his office and to hell with the consequences, but if I want to get out without repercussions, it's probably best to make as little fuss as possible."

"You're frightening me," Melissa said

"That's not my intention. Nobody wants to harm me—at least as they see harm—but . . . well, to put it simply, I don't want my relationship with you to consist of you coming to see me in that pokey little room until it becomes too tedious and you can't bear it any longer. I want us to dance. We need to dance. We need the freedom to go where we want and do what we want, if this thing between us is going to amount to something. I do want it to amount to something. I think that's worth a risk. But there really isn't any need to be afraid."

I looked her straight in the eye sockets then. She obviously wanted it to amount to something too, or at least to try it out and see if it could. She didn't want the relationship to consist of visiting me in the pokey reception room either, because she had the sense to know that that couldn't work in the long term.

"And you're wiling to take a risk, for that?" she said.

"Yes," I confirmed. "And I'd like you to help, if you will."

"Of course. What do you want me to do?"

"Pop in to see Henry and book an appointment to see me this evening—at six, not earlier. Then stand me up."

"Stand you up?"

"Yes. I need to get out without anyone noticing that I've gone. If they think I'm seeing you . . ."

"But where will you go?" she asked. "I suppose it'll be dark by then, but even so . . ."

"Just to Winding Sheet Street," I said. "Don't worry about it. Come and see me tomorrow evening, and I'll tell you all about it . . . whether it seems to be working or not."

She hesitated, and then nodded. "Okay. Good luck, then." She didn't say any more than that, or do anything at all. She knew that it was a solemn moment—and she didn't want to hug me while I was coming out in red flesh in ugly patches.

Not for much longer, though, if I have my way, I thought.

And we went back inside. She went into Henry's office. I went upstairs. I had an appointment with Sthenelais, the puppet-mistress who thought that she had all my strings securely in her virtual hand.

13

Sthenelais cut straight to the chase, like someone who had a plan fully worked out and didn't want to waste any time.

"Well, Peterkin, are you in, or out?" she demanded.

"I'm still thinking about it," I said, judiciously.

She didn't frown; in fact, she kept her ugly virtual face perfectly straight, but I knew that the mask was hiding impatience rather than disappointment. She thought that I didn't have a choice, and that my procrastination was stupid. But I was in no rush—quite the opposite, in fact. My tactics involved stalling, with all possible artistry.

"For the time being, though," I went on, "as I have no alternative, you can rely on me to be fully cooperative. With regard to my future options, as Melissa just pointed out to me, I'm sure to lose my present job, and you were right last night about my beginning to think up reasons myself why the one you're offering might have its attractions. I still want to know a lot more about it before I make a commitment, though."

"That's fair enough," she said warily. "But one thing we have to be absolutely clear about is that you have to stay with the program to the end. That's not negotiable."

That wasn't a surprise, although it was a slight disappointment. I didn't try to hide that—in fact, I tried to feign more chagrin than I actually felt. I didn't want to give her any reason to guess that I might have a plan to get out of jail without her help.

When I figured that I'd hammed it up enough, I said: "Okay then, I'll take that for granted. Let's pick up where we left it last night; what do you want me to do, exactly?"

"Firstly," she said, "I want you to pretend to remember a few things about your Larval existence—and pass them on to Dr. Charteris. It's just a little extra nudge in the direction I want his investigation to take. Lysander and Jillian have laid the groundwork, but the suggestions I've planted in their minds are tenuous. Once you've given Charteris the same story, though, he won't have any difficulty winkling confirmatory evidence out of them. If you provide some back-up for the idea that what he ought to be looking for in the background of Billy and the others is some kind of intense existential and violent crisis, he won't any longer have an atom of doubt that he might have got his fingers on a key."

"And he'll report back, and publish, and generate a few newspaper headlines," I said, slowly, although it was something I'd worked out for myself already. "And it won't just be the foremost larval expert on osteomorphism who'll spend the next five or ten years chasing wild geese, it will be everyone in his field."

"You don't know that it's a wild goose chase," the Mad Scientist pointed out. "Neither do we. It's a viable line of enquiry."

"Except that you already know that the real agent of transformation that you're testing on the others in your carefully selected sample came out of a lab at the

University, and that you already have a supposed antidote, so your primary motivation in deflecting him must be to sidetrack him from the search for the antidote, in case he should get lucky." I was just testing the water with that one, keeping another notion up my sleeve, ready for a possible ambush.

"That's just your guesswork," Sthenelais pointed out, "and Dr. Charteris has as much interest in letting the trial run its full course as we do. Don't overestimate your cleverness, Peterkin—let me do the thinking. Believe me, if you stick to the plan I've outlined for you, we'll all be better off. You and I are on the same side, and we have similar interests."

"Enabling the Ghost Faculty to rule the world?"

"That's something else that came out of your imagination—but if it were true, and if we succeeded, the world would be a lot better off for it. You're obviously a smart skelly, Peterkin, completely wasted as a school piano player. You know in your virtual heart that the Ghost Faculty isn't your enemy. Ask yourself, seriously: as an osteomorph, given the state the world is in, would you rather put your trust in us to look after the interests of all Postmortals, or give free rein to Larva paranoia? Who do you think poses the bigger danger, to you personally, and to the whole skelly species—the Ghost Faculty or the people who buried a hydrogen bomb under the Ghetto, just in case?"

She was right, I supposed, but I couldn't help feeling that if the situation were put in those terms, then the whole skelly species was caught between a rock and a hard place. I also knew that Larval farmers could make a pretty good pitch to their dairy herds and the sheep they bred for wool and the chickens they kept for eggs, in pointing out to them that it really was in their best interests to be in the byre, the fold or the coop, rather than out there with the wolves and foxes. They could even suggest to the cows, the sheep and the chickens that they were happy as they were . . . and they'd probably be correct.

I didn't have any illusions, either, about why I had been selected as the Judas goat, to play my little part in her Machiavellian scheme. Circumstances had fitted me for the role, obviously, but what had actually caused her to step out of the wall last night was the fear that I might already have picked up enough suggestions of my own actually to put Charteris on the right track rather than the wrong one. Sthenelais was playing safe, trying to neutralize a potential troublemaker by bringing him on side. And it was working. In spite of the temptations, I really couldn't see any payoff for myself, for skellies in general, or even for Dr. Charteris, in tipping him off that the Ghosts were manipulating him in order to further their own agenda—especially as I only had my own feeble guesswork to go on in trying to figure out what that agenda really was.

But I *could* see a payoff for me in sabotaging their little experiment, if my crazy idea worked. Presumably, they'd just repeat the experiment on the Outside, but they'd have had to do that anyway, and that, I figured, must be a part of the reason they were setting Charteris up with the bait they were offering him here and now. They wanted him to organize a massive field-trial with newly metamorphosed skellies and Larvae who hadn't yet undergone transition, but whose transition could somehow be anticipated. But what, exactly, was the purpose of that field trial? That was the real question—the one that I wanted to sneak up on, as cleverly as I could.

"Fair enough," I said, still stalling. "I still have questions, though."

"Of course," she said, serenely, seemingly reassured as to my cooperation, at least for the time being, and presumably ready to lie extravagantly if it seemed politic to do so. "What do you want to know?"

"I can't really assume a ghost mentality, obviously," I said, "but I can understand well enough why you think of the true and ideal human existential situation as being a ghost, and why you've made sure over the years that everyone in the Ghetto not only calls living human beings Larvae but thinks of them as larvae . . ."

"It's what they are," Sthenelais pointed out.

"I don't disagree—although they, of course, don't see it that way. But from the ghostly point of view, ghosts presumably seem to be the only true imagoes. To you, theriomorphs are just spoiled larvae, seemingly incapable of postmortal metamorphosis but subject to deleterious metamorphoses while alive. Zombies are obvious spoiled Postmortals, and were even before your failed experiment spoiled them even more. Vamps don't consider themselves to be spoiled, but that's only because they're in denial, and not always successfully, as proven by all the jokes about vampire angst. Whereas skellies, from your point of view, are just imagoes trying to be ghosts but not quite being able to get there, stuck with their awkward bones."

"I thought you wanted to ask a question?" Sthenelais prompted, presumably tired of my stating the obvious—obvious, that is, to her.

"I do." I figured that it was time to show her exactly how convoluted my mind could be now that I was actually trying. "How long have the Ghost Faculty had a reliable means of engineering human metamorphosis into osteomorphs?"

Her mask was firmly in position. She didn't show the slightest hint of surprise, so far as I could tell.

"You're guessing again," Sthenelais told me, "but I do see your point, and it is one of the matters that's at stake in the present enquiry. It's certainly not something we've been sitting on for decades, or centuries, though, for Machiavellian reasons. In fact, it's brand new and not yet tested in a properly designed experiment."

"An experiment that has to be carried out on the Outside, by Larvae—but from your point of view, carried out by Larvae who don't understand the real point of the experiment, and who think that they're testing a different hypothesis."

The mask didn't slip, and I didn't get any further compliments regarding my mental convolution. All she said was: "Yes."

"And if it works?" I said. "Given that you think skellies are just spoiled Larvae, it's not actually something you have any use for, is it?"

"It's an important step forward in scientific understanding," she told me. "You don't seem to believe me, but that really is my primary motivation."

I still didn't believe her—but I had nothing to put up in opposition. I couldn't see for the afterlife of me what use a reliable means of producing skellies would be to the Ghost Faculty . . . or even to skellies, who had no interest in trying to rule the world.

While I was pausing for further thought, she made what I assumed was a rapid modification to her own plan. "All right, Peterkin," she said. "This is a card I'm prepared to lay on the table, because it seems to me that it's yet another reason why you should want to be a part of the investigation—not just for yourself, but for your species. As you've obviously deduced, the discovery we've made hasn't been tested, for reasons of practicality. We need Dr. Charteris to test it for us, obviously, but I think you can work out for yourself why we'd rather he doesn't know what it is he's testing. We'd rather he believed that he's testing a different hypothesis, so we're trying to feed him one, so that we can test ours while he's testing his— which, as I said before, might not be a wild goose chase, but might actually throw up some interesting insights. Either way, we find out more about skelly nature and the logic of skelly existence . . . which can surely only be good for you, if you can set aside silly paranoia, as I think you already have. So, are you in?"

"Not quite," I told her, knowing that was running the risk of exasperating her, but really not giving a damn about that. "What about the other transitions? Do you have a means of engineering transitions of Larvae into vampires and zombies . . . and, for that matter, transitions of the living into werewolves?"

"Theriomorphs, no," she replied. "That one, we don't understand, and to be honest, we haven't wasted much time and effort trying. Zombies, obviously—even the Larvae found crude means of engineering that in the distant past, and it was our provisional understanding of how that process was modified in the production of vampires that led to our abortive attempt to ameliorate the zombie condition. As is perfectly obvious, though, there's not much demand for those kinds of engineering. It's rather frustrating, in fact, that although we can duplicate Nature's mistakes, we haven't yet figured out effective ways of undoing them. The premature zombie experiment was a complete disaster, not merely in itself, but in making us very wary of further projects."

"Until now."

"Until now—but as you can see, we're proceeding very carefully."

"I might say *bully for you* if I weren't caught up in it, but I am, and it's seriously inconvenient, even if I would get special privileges for helping you out. But let's put my selfishness aside for a moment and focus on yours. I'm not even certain that the vamps would necessarily agree with you that they're just nature's mistakes, and I'm pretty sure that even if they did, they wouldn't be prepared to take it for granted that you ghosts are the one and only ideal, the true human race in all its virtual purity."

"And you're not either? Speaking on behalf of osteomorphkind, that is?"

"No, I'm not."

"Because skellies are happy?" She permitted herself a sneer. I was fairly certain that it was just self-indulgence, not part of an act whose logic was far too subtle for me to figure out.

"That's an important point of consideration, from my point of view—but maybe ghosts are happy too, as you insist. The point is that skellies are skellies—just a species that exists, presumably having come into existence as one of Nature's strange random mutations. I don't see any self-evident case for thinking of us as spoiled or failed ghosts. I don't see any reason for thinking of myself, in particular, as an unfortunate abortion, simply because you were hoping that my Larva might have had the potential to become a candidate for admission to your all-virtual club if he hadn't fallen victim to stupid larval jealousy."

"We've already established that you're happy as you are, Peterkin," she said, perhaps a trifle wearily, "or as you were last week. But you can't seriously be telling me that if your larval self had had a choice between ending up as a piano and ballet teacher in a theriomorph school and a member of the Ghost Faculty, he'd have plumped for the former, and that he wouldn't have regarded getting a duplicitous shot of dope as a tragic waste of potential?"

"I don't know," I said, "because even if I could remember him, which I can't, I still wouldn't be able to put himself in his shoes—but what I do know is that you can't know either."

Sthenelais shook her virtual head. "That isn't a serious argument," she said.

"Nor is the incapacity of your imagination," I retorted.

She laughed—at least, I think she laughed; with only virtual bones and teeth, it's difficult to tell. "I truly am sorry that your Larva was poisoned prematurely," she said. "You might be only a shadow of your former self, but it seems to me to be the shadow of a mind that really might have been at home in the Ghost Faculty, given the right long-term education."

"He was just a piano-player too," I reminded her. "I have a metaphorical gut feeling that he might have disappointed you . . . just as your current experiment is going to disappoint you."

"Is it?" she said. "I don't have gut feelings myself—and neither do you, yet. I think I'll wait for the experiment to run its course before I evaluate the result. Perhaps it would be wise for you to do the same."

She was right, of course. It might, indeed, have been wise. But I wasn't aiming for wisdom. That isn't part of the skelly notion of happiness. I was being driven by unjustly frustrated amour; I wanted my happy ending, not hers—and I was prepared to be reckless in order to make a try for it.

"If you were right about it being self-evident that ghosts are the true human race, and the ideal destiny of human beings, you wouldn't have a problem, would you?" I said. "Even taking aboard your desire to be selective, and only letting the best Larvae through the filter, you could simply offer your method to the lucky few and they'd say *thank you very much*. But they don't, do they? You have to do it covertly, just as you're intending to apply your method of engineering skellies not merely covertly but deceptively. Because if Larvae were given a real choice of Postmortal conditions, they wouldn't choose ghosthood any more than they'd choose zombiedom, would they? And who knows? Maybe if their research weren't being deflected into false trails, maybe they could find some such means of choice?"

I regretted having added the last comment, thinking that perhaps I'd said too much, but she was still electing to put on a show of being amused by my folly rather than annoyed by my stubbornness, no matter how she really felt. She was humoring me. I didn't mind that at all.

"Maybe they could," she said. "They might be stupid, but there are a lot of them, and Nature's successes, as well as her mistakes, have always been produced on the try-everything-and-see-whether-something-works principle. But Larvae don't understand—they're existentially blinkered. They don't have our mature adult perspective. Nor do you, Perterkin . . . and if even you don't, what hope is there for the rest of osteomorphkind? That's why the Larvae, and your own kind, need protection and guidance. That's why it would be so much better, for everyone, if ghosts really did run the world. You *can* see that, can't you, Peterkin? The very fact that we're sitting here having this interesting psychiatric consultation proves that you *do* understand why it's in your interests, as well as mine, to see this first phase of the experiment through, so that we can steer Charteris' further steps in the direction we want them to go."

"And if it doesn't work?"

"We'll try again, and keep trying, until it does work. That's how science makes progress. But in the meantime, as you so wisely told your friend Phil yesterday, even if we did want to wipe out the skelly race—which we certainly don't—we wouldn't do it by spreading a lethal disease, let alone a disease that puts flesh on their bones. We really are doing that in order to further our understanding of the metamorphic potential of virtual flesh . . . and, of course, the metamorphic production of material flesh. We don't want anyone to suffer permanent harm, or even to suffer anything they'd mistakenly consider to be harm. We would have called for volunteers if that had been a viable option, but as you pointed out yourself, nobody would have formed a queue.

"I'll apologize to you, if you wish, for dragging you into this, but you know more than enough by now to be fully aware that circumstances beyond your or my control made you an ideal candidate for inclusion in the scheme. The rational thing for you to do now is to go with the flow, wait it out, and collect your reward for giving us what assistance you can. I'll even promise to do what little I can to ensure that your girlfriend doesn't hook up with someone else while you're on the sidelines, as long as it isn't too time-consuming. There really is a golden opportunity for you here, not just for the duration of the immediate experiment but in the longer term."

She was absolutely right. The *wise* thing to do would have been to cooperate, every inch of the way. But unlike ghosts—allegedly—skellies don't find their happiness in wisdom. They like to dance, and play their own music. I was a piano-player; I wanted my own fingers on the keys. And I wanted to be able to build my relationship with Melisa in my own way, in my own time, without any outside interference. And given that I had an experiment of my own that I wanted to try, there was no way I was going to be put off, unless and until it failed. If it did fail there would be time enough to settle for being wise, from a ghostly point of view.

So, what I said to Sthenelais was: "I still have to think about it. But in the meantime, as I said before, I'll cooperate."

I think that she thought that I was just putting on a show, because I didn't want to back down too easily, as a matter of foolish pride.

"Well," she said judiciously, "I suppose there's no such thing as too much thinking. If you really need more time to see the obvious, take it. After all, you'll be here for some time yet."

"So it seems," I said, while thinking: *Not if I can help it, you supercilious bitch.* But I smiled, confident that no matter how sharp-sighted a ghost she was, she couldn't possibly tell how fake that gleaming white skelly smile was.

14

As expected, Dr. Charteris called me into his office when my pretended hypnotherapy session with Sthenelais ended, eager to know whether I'd remembered anything.

"I can't be certain," I told him, dutifully, as I had been requested to do, "but I certainly have a strong feeling that my Larva didn't commit suicide—that I was murdered. Murdered by Lysander Link, I think . . . but I don't have anything at all against Lysander as he is now, an entirely different person."

The doctor nodded. "That's interesting, and it could be something of a breakthrough," he told me, hypocritically. "We really don't have any idea why some humans acquire Postmortality, or why, when they do, they acquire the particular postmortal conditions they do. There have always been legends, of course, linking ghosts with traumatic experiences in life, particularly murder, but there isn't even a legendary connection of that kind with osteomorphs. I thought for a moment, when the triad consisting of you, Jillian and Lysander first leapt to my attention, that the crucial link might be the music, but when Sthenelais began to uncover these fugitive memory traces . . . it might not only provide an indicator to identifying humans that are likely to undergo postmortal metamorphoses, but, perhaps more importantly, offer us a better understanding of what's happening to you and the others. The flesh you're putting on might be a kind of physical memory trace, you see."

"I suppose it might" I agreed. *And pigs might fly*, I thought.

"Testing the hypothesis will be fiendishly difficult, of course," he said. "It depends, to some extent, on how many more cases turn up spontaneously in the Ghetto, but no matter how many or how few there are, the real testing will have to be done Outside, and that will create all kinds of political difficulties. The work I've been doing with early Postmortals has always been dogged by difficulties, as you can probably imagine."

"Not really," I said. "Once we're in the Ghetto, we don't really have much idea of what goes on Outside, except for what we see on TV—which is obviously a severely censored and heavily biased picture. Apparently, there are new communication technologies in use out there that we don't have at all, in case our malcontents contrive to find common cause with Larval malcontents, and stir up trouble on both sides of the wall."

"That's true," he agreed. "It's completely unnecessary, in my opinion, but the pattern of human fears, and political responses to them, is a complicated matter. You and I know that there's absolutely no reason for the living to be frightened of osteomorphs, for instance, and that their visceral reaction to seeing animated skeletons is simply a hangover of ancient superstition. If I can contrive a large-scale field experiment tracking hypothetical anticipations of osteomorphic metamorphoses, that might actually help to put a dent in popular prejudice, if the publicity is handled delicately. And the same goes for the possibility that osteomorphs are able to put on flesh again. I know that seems like a horrible prospect to you, but you can understand, I think, why it might seem like a welcome possibility to mortals?"

"I can see that it requires delicate publicity," I agreed, "both in and out of the Ghetto. But you said this morning that it might only be a temporary condition—that it might get better . . . better from our point of view, that is . . . of its own accord. Did you mean that, or were you just trying to maintain morale?"

"No, there is some historical evidence, albeit slight, and Sthenelais seems quite willing to take it seriously. She seems optimistic, too, that the members of the Ghost Faculty to whom we've sent samples might be able to identify a means of reversing the process, given time. It might take months, though, in her estimation."

"I hope her optimism turns out to be justified," I said, keeping my tone carefully neutral. "And it will make your field experiment even more interesting, I suppose?"

"It would certainly make it more complicated—but the essential thing is to find reliable indicators to inform us of the likelihood of particular mortals acquiring Postmortal potential. Not that it will delight those that we might be able to identify in advance, alas . . . not in the beginning, at any rate. It might take a long time to persuade people that reincarnation as an osteomorph really is quite an attractive prospect, as an alternative to permanent death. Although, of course . . ."

He stopped.

"Of course . . . ?" I prompted.

He hesitated. "Well, it has occurred to me that if the Ghost Faculty researchers can find a way to dissolve the material flesh that you and our unfortunate fellow patients are developing, it's not impossible that it might go further."

"I can't see what you mean," I lied.

"I mean that if the Ghost Faculty find a way of converting your adventitious material flesh back into a virtual state, it might also work on bone."

"You mean that it might become possible for skellies to metamorphose into ghosts?"

"There is a school of thought, as you probably know, especially among the Ghost community, that such a process would be a curative process—a means of completing a metamorphosis that has stalled."

"Skellies wouldn't see it that way," I said. "We don't want meat on our bones, but we certainly don't want to give up our bones."

"Yes, I know," the doctor agreed. "That's understandable."

"Ghosts can't dance," I said. "They think they can, but they can't. Lykes think that they can dance too—they even have ballet lessons at the school—but it's not *really* dancing."

He seemed dubious, as one might expect. Larvae, after all, invented dancing, and are presumably convinced that what skellies do isn't *really* dancing. But what do they know? They're only Larvae, after all: caterpillars with delusions of grandeur.

"The piano has been set up in the common room, by the way," he said. "You and Lysander will be able to play in concert tonight, if your bruised wrist is up to it. I hear you had quite an active session last night."

"Yes," I confirmed. "We did."

"But you'll want to see your girlfriend first, I expect?"

"Hopefully," I said, even though I had already told her that I had other plans, and that visiting hours were a better time for me to slip out unobserved than the middle of the night, because the staff wouldn't be on guard and there would be plenty of people about, including numerous people clad in cloaks and hoods.

"I realize that to you, Peterkin, this must seem a terrible misfortune," Dr. Charteris said, "but you've been a real godsend to the investigation, first by confirming my hypothesis, and then by helping to elaborate it with the aid of your recovered memories."

"Glad to be of help," I said, in a tone whose subtle irony was easy for him to miss.

"There might be a lot of mileage in my new hypothesis," he said. "The idea that Postmortal events . . . perhaps even the Postmortal condition itself . . . might be a kind of posthumous psychosomatic effect of emotional trauma . . . it's a whole new way of looking at things."

"As you say, there might be a lot of mileage in it," I agreed. "For you and many others. Including members of the Ghost Faculty, of course."

"Yes, I think Sthenelais is genuinely excited about it . . . although her first priority, obviously, has to be discovering means of controlling transitions between real and virtual flesh. That's the holy grail of all Postmortal research."

"The road to paradise," I said, dutifully. "But it's the other one, isn't it, that's paved with good intentions?"

He looked at me quizzically, unable to follow my drift—but he settled for treating it as a witticism. "So they say," he agreed. "Tradition has always represented the road to paradise as a steep climb beset with thorns. That certainly seems to have been the case . . . but our ideas of paradise have changed quite markedly since the discovery of the actual Postmortal conditions . . . or, more accurately, the acceptance by science of their reality. The idea of choirs of disembodied spirits singing the praises of God isn't really consonant with what we now know about the reality of ghosts."

"Nor is the idea of an Inferno of eternal torment, mercifully," I said, although I wasn't absolutely convinced that if the Ghost Faculty ever did get to rule and reorganize the world with a virtual hand in an iron glove, it would be more akin to paradise than hell, at least from the Larval point of view.

"Mercifully," echoed Dr. Charteris. He glanced at the clock. "You'd better go, now, though, if you're expecting a visitor. Thanks for all your help—I really appreciate it."

"No trouble," I assured him. "Anything I can do . . ."

And I left it at that.

As I came out of my bedroom wearing my cloak, with my hood already pulled up, I ran into Billy and Helen, similarly clad.

"You too, eh, son?" said Billy. "It's a pain, isn't it? Do you think we'll ever be able to show our faces to our friends again?"

"Oh, I think so," I said. "I've just seen the Doctor, and he seems quite optimistic."

"He's always optimistic," said Helen. "It's easy for him—he likes his flesh, and he's quite comfortable in it. He has no idea how ugly he is, poor thing."

"I think they do know, really," said Billy. "They only pretend to think that naked skulls are horrible. They're like vamps—they know that they're monsters but they put on that calculated arrogance to hide their shame. The Larvae know that they're ugly, but their pride won't let them admit it."

"Well, his optimism had better stop short of telling me I look beautiful when my face is fully grown," said Helen, "if he doesn't want his eyes scratched out by these." She held up her hand, where material fingernails were beginning to become manifest. They still looked soft to me, however, incapable as yet of scratching anything.

The three of us went downstairs in line. There was another hooded figure in the corridor, evidently waiting for a visitor who hadn't yet arrived. I was delighted to observe that it could have been anyone. Adelaide was at her station and Henry was in his office.

Helen went in to see the orderly.

"I'm going to step outside," Billy muttered. "At least it's dark out there. It's not cold, either—if the lady comes, I might just take her into a corner of the courtyard. How about you?"

"Sounds like a good idea to me," I agreed. "I'm still at the stage of trying to impress . . . the last thing I want is to make the poor girl feel sick."

"Hang on in there, son," said the well-meaning hero. "There must be a dozen things I haven't thought of yet, as well as all the chemicals with unpronounceable names that Charteris and his cancer specialist are trying out. If there's something that works, we'll find it."

"I hope so," I said. "I truly hope so."

"Here comes mine," he said, adjusting his hood, as a female skelly came through the open gate, sidling with the slightly furtive gait of someone who would rather not be seen entering a place where all hope was in the process of being abandoned. "I hope yours isn't too long coming." It didn't take a genius to work out from his tone that what he was really hoping for, on my behalf, was that I wouldn't simply be stood up. I was grateful for the sympathy.

I reached behind my head and adjusted my own hood. Then I struck an expectant pose, until Billy, following his own suggestion, had taken his visitor away to a quiet corner, and was no longer paying attention. Nor was anybody else, so far as I could tell, and I was fairly confident that no one was lurking inside a nearby wall, keeping me under surveillance.

I slipped outside, and moved away rapidly, avoiding the streetlights as much as possible.

I have to admit that I wasn't confident. In fact, every step I took seemed to reinforce the suspicion that my idea was utterly ludicrous. I tried to tell myself that if it weren't ludicrous, Billy would have tried it, but it wasn't exactly a convincing argument. He had his imaginative limitations. So did Leopold Charteris. They were both ingenious, in their own ways, but they were blinkered thinkers with relatively narrow fields of focus. Sthenelais was banking on that.

I was also scared. The place for which I was heading was dangerous, and the people to whom I was going to address myself had already proved that they were worse than dangerous, because they were morons as well—but needs must when the devil drives, as they say. If I were going to be a hero, I could hardly expect it to be easy. Fear came with the métier, and I simply had to live with it.

At least I'm doing something, I told myself, sternly. *At least I'm not settling meekly for being a Ghost Faculty pawn, obediently pushing forward, not knowing whether I'm just a sacrifice within the pattern of a game beyond my understanding. At least I'm trying to be a player.*

That was, after all, what I was destined to be, with or without a piano. Peterkin had once been Peter Strangland, certified virtuoso, potential genius and penciled-in candidate for the Ghost Faculty. I wasn't him—I was a very different person, in fact—but even so, I felt a certain twinge of strange pride at the idea that he might have approved of me, and might even have been able to think that perhaps he hadn't died entirely in vain.

As I went down Winding Sheet Street, I felt a little weak at the knees, but I consoled myself with the thought that it was a thoroughly bony sort of weakness; my legs hadn't yet begun to turn to jelly.

The zombie brothers were hanging around the intersection halfway down the street, as was their habit, but they didn't have their friends with them as yet. It was dark, still being only the first week in March, but it was still a little early for making nocturnal mischief. There was no one they needed to impress, for the moment.

They made as if to walk away again, but I was much quicker over the ground than they were, and they didn't want to seem like the kind of zombies who'd run away from a mere skelly, so when I caught them up they turned to face me, ready to argue the toss.

"I very nearly got run over by that train the other night," I said to the younger one.

It was the older one who answered: "Didn't know there was a train coming," he whined. "Thought you'd 'ave plenty of time to get free. It was just a *joke*."

"I figured that," I said. "It worked. Scared me to Life. Did you know that bony folk can be scared back to Life?"

I lowered my hood, secure in the knowledge that they weren't going to be horrified by the sight of a thin layer of something that still looked more like red paint than flesh growing on a skelly's cheekbones.

"That's just an urban legend," the younger zombie said. "It can't really happen. The Undead can't go back to Life. That's just paint."

"No, it's real," I said. I held up my wrist and let the sleeve fall back, in order to display the worst of the patches. They weren't impressed, but that was only to be expected.

"T'ain't natural," admitted the older of the two, grudgingly.

"But it's not our fault," added the younger.

"Well, you weren't to know what would happen, that's true," I conceded. "Still, I figured that as your joke so nearly went sour, you might be willing to do me a small favor."

The younger brother was still looking at my fuzzy wrist. "Are you really turning into a zombie?" he asked.

"Can't tell yet," I replied, suppressing an urge to say *Almighty Chance forbid!* "I must confess, though, that I don't really want to find out."

The older of the two shook his head stubbornly. "'T'aint natural," he said again. Coming from someone whose notion of "natural" included his own putrescent presence, the judgment seemed to me to be a trifle excessive.

"Strange things happen to all kinds of folk," I told him, patiently. "Even to zombies. Do you happen to know any zombies that strange things have happened to?"

"Like what?" asked the elder brother, frowning at the very notion of anything happening to a zombie qualifying as strange.

"Do you know what a notifiable disease is?" I asked.

"Of course we do," said the younger. "We're not stupid."

I was prepared to believe that the notion of a notifiable disease was familiar to him, if only as a rule to be avoided at all costs.

"Well," I said, "this red stain is a notifiable disease, and, being stupidly law-abiding, I went and notified it. Zombies, so I've heard, know better than to do that. Right?"

"What's it to you?" the younger zombie demanded, suspiciously. "It's no skin off your nose, is it? If you had a nose, that is . . . and skin." The additions were made with a frown rather than a grin; the kid wasn't getting any smarter, but he was still smart enough to know that he was losing his ability even to see jokes, let alone make them.

"Well, that's true," I said. "I don't have a nose, or skin. You two have a fine pair of noses—but there are zombies that don't, aren't there? There are zombies who don't have much in the way of skin, either."

"Is there a point to all this?" the younger brother asked.

"Yes there is," I said, trying to be patient, because I didn't want to seem too eager. "As I said, I think that you ought to figure that you owe me one, for nearly getting me killed, and it just so happens that there's a little favor you might be able to do me. A very little one—no skin off your nose, as you put it so elegantly. I thought that it might make you rest a little easier in your consciences."

The older brother wasn't following my argument at all, and probably hadn't enough conscience left to stir a feather, but the younger one could at least see the moral point. He was the one who'd nearly got me killed, if only by not protesting when he'd had the chance and the inclination to do so, and by not coming back to help me free myself when his mates wandered away. He knew that it hadn't been a neighborly thing to do, given that we really were all Postmortals, and had to live together whether we liked it or not. Even zombies didn't want to live in a neighborhood so exclusive that the only other folk willing to share it with them are other zombies.

"What do you want?" he said, tiredly.

I told him.

He shook his head—not because he was saying no but because he thought it was a seriously weird request.

"I'm not taking you," the zombie said. "It's not decent. But I suppose I could give you an address. What you do with it is your business, right? Nothing to do with us, if anyone should ask."

"Absolutely," I agreed. I didn't say that my lips were sealed, because I didn't think he'd get the joke.

"What address?" the older brother asked, still lagging way behind.

The younger brother shook his head. "Don't worry about it," he said to his sibling: To me, he added: "You might have to hurry. You won't get any sense out of her, but you won't be disturbed."

"I understand that," I assured him, after the barest hesitation over the fact that he'd said *she* rather than *he*. "Just give me the address, will you?"

The older brother still looked puzzled, almost as if he'd forgotten what an address was. The younger told me without any further ado, though, adding: "This makes us even, right—whether you get what you're expecting or not? No hard feelings?"

"None at all," I assured him, insincerely.

15

I didn't go down the hill immediately; first I went into 227 in order to have a wash. There were three recorded messages waiting on the answerphone, but I didn't bother to play them back. When the phone actually rang as I came out of the bathroom carrying a couple of empty salt jars, though, the surprise made my bones rattle. If I'd been a little further along in the progress of my disease, I'd probably have jumped out of my skin. Then I rattled again as the door to the vestibule opened and someone came in. For a moment, I thought that my absence from the clinic had been noticed, and that someone had come to fetch me back. But that was a false alarm.

"Melissa!" I said. "What are you doing here?"

"Looking for you," she replied, logically enough. "You said you'd be coming here, but I didn't ring the bell because I thought you might not want anyone else to know you were here."

I realized that she'd jumped to the wrong conclusion when I'd named the street as my objective for the evening excursion. I chided myself for my carelessness, but not very hard. Truth to tell, I was glad to see her. It was a pity that I was in a hurry.

"I can't stop," I said, regretfully. "I'm on my way . . . somewhere else."

"I'll come with you."

"That's not a good idea. Where I'm going is no place for . . . someone like you."

"What's that supposed to mean?"

"I'm going down the hill," I said. "All the way down."

"Ah," she said. She was much better at putting two and two together than the older zombie. "You're trying to catch something, aren't you? To fight disease with disease?"

"That's right," I said. "The mother of all nasty bacterial cocktails—something that can strip the flesh off bones like a hive of soldier ants. As I said before, it might not work . . . but I figure that it's worth a try. It's best if I do it alone, though. Collecting it won't be pleasant. Please, Melissa."

She thought about it. I was grateful to her for almost insisting, because it demonstrated a definite enthusiasm for our fledgling relationship, but I was also grateful to her for stopping short, because I felt the same way, and I didn't want her to remember that our first real date had been in the Ditch at the bottom end of Winding Sheet Street, in the utmost depths of zombietown.

"Okay," she said. "But I'll come to see you tomorrow evening. You said I could."

"Thanks," I said. "By then, I might have some idea as to whether it's working—but be careful to keep your distance. Best keep the number of carriers to a minimum."

She hesitated before leaving, and almost made a speech, but in the end she only said: "Good luck, Peterkin. I'll keep my phalanges crossed."

"Thanks," I said, very sincerely.

When the door closed behind her again, I went to look for a sharp knife and a bag to carry the jars in. I threw a couple of ballpoint pens into the bag along with the empty jars.

It didn't take me long to walk down to the very bottom of the hill; it wasn't far, and the necessary strides seemed almost effortless, even though the slope became shallower. Even though zombies have squishy eyes, the street lighting was very poor; it felt like a different, much darker world than the brightly lit crest of the hill. There were no skellies living way down here. Even the healthier zombies—insofar as you could describe any zombie as healthy—didn't like coming down here. When the older of the two brothers was eventually carried down into the Ditch, his younger sibling wouldn't make a habit of visiting him. Even though zombies have considerably stronger kinship ties than vamps or lykes, the ties in question aren't strong enough to overcome the worst of zombie dreads and superstitions.

I found the address that the teen had given me without any difficulty. I didn't bother to knock on the door. There was no lock on it, so I had no difficulty getting in.

The tenant was in bed. There were no curtains over the widow, but it was still almost pitch dark. Another zombie wouldn't have been able to see a thing, but I had virtual vision, and I could make her out well enough. The lack of distinction wasn't all due to my eyesight, by any means. She didn't blink—but her eyes did move in their sockets, to demonstrate that the afterlife was still working away inside her useless flesh.

I sat down on the chair beside the bed, resolutely ignoring the condition of the upholstery—not to mention the condition of the bedcover, the carpet and the grimy walls.

I couldn't help remembering the younger of the brothers saying "no skin off my nose" in the faint hope of insulting my nature. As I'd pointed out by way of reply, zombies weren't always capable of preserving their own noses, or their own skin. This one still had a lot more flesh left than poor Lysander had yet grown, but what she had was in *much* worse condition than his. It was still possible to make out muscles and blood vessels, but the distinction was fading. Most zombies come in various shades of gray, but I suspected that this one was probably a very particular purple color.

"I'm sorry to intrude. Ma'am," I said, because I thought I ought to be polite, and that she would probably appreciate it if, by any chance, she could hear and understand me. "My name's Peterkin." I remembered a phrase that I had flung at Sthenelais with righteous resentment: *informed consent*. The foundation-stone of medical ethics.

Well, I thought, *this is a medical matter, after all. I'm a researcher now, if not a fully fledged Mad Scientist.*

It wasn't an entirely serious thought, but it was serious enough. Even though she was a zombie—the kind of zombie that even other zombies wouldn't go near—I felt that I owed it to her at least to try to tell her what I was doing, and why. It didn't matter that she was a mindless flesh-eating monster, or that a gang of her fresher cousins had wired me to a railway track in the early hours of Sunday morning. It didn't even matter that I couldn't do her any actual bodily harm, and might be reckoned to be doing her a favor, albeit one as tiny as the one the teen had done for me. I still felt that I ought to ask, and to be polite.

"There's a possibility that you can help me," I said, "if you wouldn't mind. I'm in need of a pound of flesh—not just any flesh, but a very particular kind of flesh . . . a kind of flesh that's rather rare, even way down here at the bottom end of Winding Sheet Street. You have a fairly abundant supply, as it happens, and I'd like to cut it from your body, if you wouldn't mind. I don't think it'll hurt you—either in the sense that the cutting will be painful, or in the sense that the wound will do you any harm. I can't claim to be any kind of expert, but I suspect that if you were a Larval person in a hospital, the surgeons might have made a similar incision some time ago, in the hope of doing you some good. We both know that nothing I can do now could possibly do you any good, so I won't try to pretend that there's anything altruistic in what I want to do—but I honestly don't think it can hurt you.

"I know that you probably can't understand me, and may not even be able to hear me, but I need to explain what I'm doing, if only for my own benefit, so I hope you'll bear with me for a few minutes more. You see, I have an embarrassing condition—a sort of disease. I'm growing flesh. That might not sound like a terrible thing to you, and probably wouldn't to anyone, except a skelly, but to us . . . well, let's just say that it's a uniquely horrible thought. I've seen some other people that have it, and they've tried all the things that immediately spring to mind: cutting it off; scrubbing it off; burning it off. They've tried acids and alkalis, alcohol and ammonia. All those treatments make inroads into the symptoms, but only temporarily. It keeps coming back.

"I thought of a different approach, but I figured I'd better try it out by myself rather than throwing it on the table, because . . . well, the doctor who's in charge of our treatment is a Larva, and he might not be prepared to take the risk, even if he knew where to get a supply, and his collaborator is a Ghost—a member of the Ghost Faculty, no less—and she has her own agenda, which might make her more liable to stop me than help me. So here I am.

"I need something extremely inimical to flesh—something that won't only get rid of the unnatural growth temporarily, but might be capable of lingering tenaciously in the bone, hopefully long enough to prevent it coming back. What skelly sufferers from this kind of plague need, you see, is to become carriers of a jealous kind of life that can and will prevent anything more substantial getting a foothold in their substance. As soon as I thought of that, the words *gangrene* and *necrotizing fasciitis* immediately sprang to mind, but I'm not fussy—any cocktail of seriously aggressive flesh-eating bacteria would probably do.

"I don't suppose zombies are any more anxious to talk about their existential woes than skellies are, even to one another, but zombies don't have the advantage of not needing to eat. The habits and weaknesses of your kind tend to be an object of urgent interest and concern to your potential victims, so they get a lot more publicity—publicity that even gets into skelly gossip. We know that zombie Postmortality is a fleeting phenomenon—even more fleeting than life—because zombie flesh tends to be even more prone to all the shocks that flesh is heir to than the original model. We know, too, that zombies suffer from the same diseases as Larvae, only more so; they don't die of them in quite the same way, because they're already Postmortal, but the worst such afflictions literally rot the flesh on zombie bones, eventually reducing it to mere slime. So I figured that if I could find a zombie at exactly the right point in his—I mean her—career, she might be willing and able to help me out.

"I'll try it on myself first, of course, and offer some to Billy, and maybe Jillian and Lysander. If it works, and works demonstrably, there'll be no way that Charteris and Sthenelais will be able to refuse it to the others. The probability is that they'll be able to make a culture and grow it in a lab—but if not, the city has no shortage of zombies, has it? And the time comes when every one of them is so far dissolved that he—or she—can no longer feed. At which point . . . well, it's not for me to say when the wielding of a knife like mine is a kindness, but it's certainly no injury. I didn't tell the boys who told me where to find you what I was going to do, but that was more to spare their fugitive feelings than to get them back for tying me to a railway line. There's really nothing malicious in my intention. Do you think you could possibly blink your eyes to let me know that it's okay?"

The gaze of the staring eyes had never left my face. They weren't incapable of movement yet—but they didn't blink either. The likelihood was that she hadn't been able to understand a word I'd said. Her brain had probably turned to gray goo.

I thought about it for a minute, and realized that there was something else I could try—something else I ought to try, before getting on with the job. It was obvious, and I would certainly have thought of it earlier if my mind hadn't shied away from the thought as if by reflex action.

I looked at the fingers of my left hand, where I'd first noticed the alien growth, and where it seemed to be thickest.

She had no nose but she still had lips, and a tongue. I eased my fingers into her mouth, and invited her to suck.

She didn't respond immediately, but her mouth eventually got a grip, if only by virtue of reflex action.

"Maybe nobody's thought of this up at the quarantine unit," I said. "If they have, they've probably kept quiet about it. If you think about it, though, zombies and my kind of skelly are kind of made for one another. It would never work as a meaningful relationship, though—not on any kind of routine basis. All I want from you is a means of stopping the growth and curing the disease, but your fresher friends wouldn't see it that way, would they? They wouldn't want to stop it—they'd want to promote it. They'd want it to keep on growing, the thicker and quicker the better. I wouldn't want to be some zombie family's private meat factory, and nor would any other skelly—even one who couldn't bear to be seen by others of their own kind. This is a one-off trade. You take my unwanted flesh; I take yours. You don't tell anyone; I only tell people who'll be *extremely* anxious to keep the secret. No one will ever know who doesn't *need* to know. It's all a bit primitive—maybe a bit fourteenth-century—but if so, that gives us cause to hope that the fix might work for a little longer than a lifetime, even in a world where there's too much reckless use of antibiotics."

I looked around then, suddenly anxious that I'd been utterly stupid, and that I'd find the younger of the two zombie brothers standing exultantly in the doorway, having just possessed himself of knowledge that might make him a hero to his folk—but he wasn't there. Even if he'd worked out what it was I intended to do with the information he'd given me, as he probably had, he hadn't been able to bring himself to come down to the address he'd given me in order to confirm his hypothesis. As he'd said himself, it wasn't decent.

The stricken zombie woman licked my phalanges clean.

Then she blinked. It might have been a reflex action, signifying nothing—or it might not. It might not have been consent, in any meaningful sense . . . but it might have. Perhaps, she was even glad to help out.

Either way, I took my pound of gangrenous flesh, and I only spilled a few sluggish drops of foul black blood. Then I left, and I didn't look back.

16

By the time I got back, it was way past seven, and Henry was pacing up and down in the corridor of the "clinic." I had the jars hidden under my cloak.

"Where the hell have you been?" he demanded.

"I went for a walk," I told him, as if it were the most natural thing in the world.

"You didn't have permission," he objected.

"I didn't need permission," I reminded him. "I'm a free agent. It's dark." I didn't have to explain why that was a relevant issue.

I tipped my hood back to expose my face, and stared at him. He was a Larva; he'd been living with skellies for at least a week, but he's probably spent most of that time avoiding looking at them, to the extent that he could, and they'd been polite enough not to confront him. He couldn't meet my eyeless stare.

"They're waiting for you upstairs," he said, sullenly. "They want you to play the piano."

"Well, they would, wouldn't they?" I said. "That's what I do." And I strode past him and went up the stairs. He didn't move.

I went to my room first, and hid one of the jars there. Then I took the tips and the ink cylinders out of the ballpoint pens, filled the empty cases with flesh from the other jar and put the plastic caps over the ends of the cases in order to provide a seal of sorts. I slipped them into a roll of sheet music.

When I arrived, Lysander was sawing away, and the dance, although not yet in full swing, was at least building up a frantic enthusiasm. Nobody rushed to greet me, and only a couple of them even glanced in my direction. The light was subdued, there being no one in the common room except skellies. I was determined to move in mysterious ways, however, just in case the walls had eyes.

I palmed one of the pen-cases to Billy, and murmured: "It might not work, but if you want to give it a try, you're welcome. Don't make it obvious."

He looked at me with a puzzled expression, but he had seen enough TV drama to know that when someone slips something to you in that fashion, it's probably best to play along.

"Thanks," he muttered. He didn't have to ask what it was that I'd slipped him. He knew what it had to be for.

I hesitated as to what to do with the second case for a little while, because there didn't seem to be any immediate prospect of getting it to Lysander unobtrusively, but in the end I figured that Jillian was the most likely one to go along with the secrecy game in any case, so I slipped it to her with the same invitation.

I was right—she did go along with it. Like Billy, she had probably figured when I was late back that I must be up to something, and there was only one thing that I could possibly be up to. She had sense enough not to question the covert nature of the exchange.

Then I went to sit down at the piano, and joined in with the music. My left hand was stiff, and I didn't think I'd be able to play for long, even sparing the hand as much as I could, but I thought that I ought to make the effort.

The dancing wasn't as frenzied as it had been the previous evening, although it was by no means staid. I was far short of my best, but nobody cared that I wasn't in top form. I did what I was supposed to do. I couldn't lose myself in the music, though; had I been able to join the dance, I wouldn't have been able to lose myself in that either.

When I went back to my room, Sthenelais was waiting for me, holding the jar from which I'd taken the two samples in her ghostly hand.

"What is it?" she asked, tiredly.

"Rotting zombie flesh," I told her. There didn't seem to be any point in dissimulation. She was too late, and she couldn't be in two places at once.

"Why?" Her voice sounded tired rather than angry.

"Because I wanted to get rid of this," I said, holding up my wrist.

"I know that," she said. "I mean, why didn't you mention it to me, or Dr. Charteris, so that we could discuss the matter?"

"I didn't think that was the way things were done around here," I told her. "I thought sneaky and underhanded were standard practice."

"I trusted you," she said.

"Bullshit. You thought you had me securely under your thumb. You weren't wrong—but I figured that I might as well use what wiggle room I had left. I know that it might not work, but it can't do any harm, can it?"

"You don't know that," she said. "It can't do any harm to me, but you . . . bone is living tissue, as you know full well, and you know that zombies eventually rot away completely. So yes, it might do harm, even to you and your friends. I'll have to warn Dr. Charteris and the living assistants to be careful, of course, but we probably have the resources to deal with any accidental infection. Even so . . ."

"If it does work," I pointed out, "all Dr. Charteris has to do is smile at his patients and say 'I told you so.' After all, he has been telling us so. You and he can still go ahead with phase two on the Outside. You'll have to wait a while before tracking the regeneration process to whatever culmination you have in mind, but your plan for world domination is a centuries-long affair, and a brief hitch like this one is a drop in the ocean . . . assuming that it does turn out to be a hitch."

"Even so," she repeated, "I have to say, Peterkin, that I'm disappointed in you."

"Perhaps you expected too much," I said, lightly.

"Evidently. Do you have any other petty acts of treason in mind?"

"You mean, am I going to tell Charteris that you've been playing him for a mug? No, I don't think so. Actually, he seems to me to be smart enough to figure it out for himself. You might be underestimating him, too. Easily done, I think, when you think you're so clever that no one else can ever begin to compare."

"Indeed. On the other hand, I can't help suggesting to you that you might be overestimating yourself. If this stuff does turn out to be nasty enough to rot your bones as well as your superfluous flesh, everyone will turn on you, inside the clinic and out."

"It's a risk," I admitted. "But as you say, you already have the resources to combat necrotizing fasciitis and gangrene, while your artificial disease is another matter."

"It's not a disease. I thought you, at least, might have been able to cultivate enough curiosity to be interested in seeing the growth process through to the end, especially as I've told you that I have an antidote."

That's one of the things that encouraged me to try it," I said. "I figured that if you had an antidote, however esoteric it might be, there must be others. As you and Charteris seemed narrowly focused on chemical agents, I thought that biological was the way to go. At least a little of the credit ought to fall to you."

"I'll pass, if you don't mind. You'll forgive me if I refrain from congratulating you, even if it works. You've really let me down, you know—not to mention the cause of science. I had such high hopes of you." She contrived a sigh, of sorts, but her heart wasn't in the mimicry.

"And they call me an optimist," I said, sarcastically. "Maybe you, at least, should have been willing to try the classic mad scientist's ploy of testing the treatment out on yourself before victimizing a gang of innocent skellies. Didn't you have curiosity enough to wonder what you might become if your virtual flesh were remetamorphosed into squishy flesh?"

"We tried," she said. "Not on me, admittedly, or any member of the Faculty, but we did try the process on ghost flesh. It needs the bone, apparently, as an anchorage. It had to be osteomorphs—why that's the case is one of the things we were hoping to figure out, with your help."

"Our involuntary, uninformed help."

"I did inform you, albeit a trifle belatedly. Look how that turned out. I should have kept quiet."

"The result would have been the same, I assure you. It wouldn't even have made any difference if you'd left me out of your sample. Someone would have thought of it. It was just a matter of time. You should have skipped phase one entirely, and gone Outside from the start, using newly metamorphosed skellies who didn't even know that regenerating flesh was unusual or terrible."

"You have no idea what the political difficulties of doing that would have been . . . and will be, now that we're going to have to take the investigation outside the walls. Still, at least you fed Charteris the fake memory. That should help to keep his mind focused, and give him a boost to his motivation. He's going to need all the encouragement he can get."

She was right; I didn't have any idea what kind of political difficulties she and Charteris were going to run into Outside, if my antidote worked and fouled up their preliminary field test—but that wasn't my fault. It was the fault of the wise heads who subjected the information flowing into the Ghetto go strict filtration and censorship.

"Well," I told her, "there's nothing to do now but wait and see what happens—and hope for whatever seems to us to be hopeful."

"If you'd only been able to continue to act rationally," she said, regretfully, "I wouldn't have to hope. I didn't realize how smitten you were with that idiotic girl, and how crazy it would drive you. Such a ridiculous thing to make you throw a spanner in the works. You're supposed to be beyond all that—all ghost, damn it, but for the bones. How can virtual flesh be so frail and perverse?"

"Good question," I said. "Don't look to me for an answer, though. I'm just a piano-player. You're the scientific genius. How *can* virtual flesh be so frail and perverse?"

"Peter Strangland could have been *anything*," the Ghost murmured, "if that idiot Lysander Link hadn't been besotted with that stupid oboe player. Bizarre!"

"Doubtless things will be far better organized if the Ghost Faculty ever does get to rule the world," I said. "But you'll never be able to do without Larvae, even if you or they decide that postmortals and theriomorphs are surplus to requirements. And in the meantime . . . Can I get some sleep now? I feel a little queasy; but with luck, I might feel a lot better in the morning."

She sighed, but at least she had the grace to say: "I suppose I ought to hope you're right, for your sake . . . but, guts or no guts, I have a bad feeling about this."

I resisted the temptation to say: "Good." After all, she was taking it like a gentlewoman, not threatening to have me hung, drawn and quartered for disobeying Ghost Faculty orders.

She was a ghost though. She couldn't let me have the last word.

"This isn't over, Peterkin," she told me. "Whether this crazy cocktail works or not, this isn't over."

"If it does work," I assured her, "it's over for me. If I can get rid of this vile disease—by which I mean your nasty mess, not mine, there's no way I'm going to involve myself any further with the Ghost Faculty. Live and let live is my motto."

"You can't bury your head in the sand forever, Peterkin. Eventually, things are going to go sour, Inside and Outside. There will come a time—maybe not for ten or twenty years, but you have young bones and you're a relatively recent arrival in the Ghetto, so it will surely be in your afterlifetime—when skellies are going to need all the help that the Faculty can give them, based on all the knowledge we can acquire in the interim. You should have stayed with the program. Maybe you won't have any choice . . . but either way, *it isn't over.*"

I knew that she was probably right, and that there might come a time down the line when I would regret not throwing in my lot with the Faculty . . . but in the short term, nothing mattered to me but Melissa. Love excuses everything, for those capable of feeling it.

"If you're waiting for an apology," I told her, "you'll be disappointed . . . again."

She shook her virtual head, miming sorrow. Then she stepped through the wall, without bothering to say goodnight.

17

If the plan hadn't worked, of course, there's no way in the world that I'd ever have told *anyone* this story, so you won't be surprised to learn that it did. The bacteria I'd plundered from the melting zombie attacked the unwelcome flesh with gusto. Within a matter of days, I was clean. So was Jillian. Billy took a little longer, but he got there. The rest followed in their turn. Dr. Charteris had no alternative but to pretend to be delighted.

I wasn't back at the Palais de Danse Macabre by Saturday, but I was the Saturday after, as bright as a brand new button. Melissa and I danced all night, and it was fabulous. We had a meaningful relationship by then, and then some, and the inside of my skull felt ten times better than anything anyone with a squishy brain could possibly imagine.

We're still together now, although Phil and Salome split up after a brief fling, and Melissa seems to be harboring a paranoid suspicion that Salome is always looking for the slightest opportunity to steal me from her. They're still best friends, though.

I lost my job at the school, but I didn't really mind. I got another easily enough, thanks to Lysander, playing in the Carillon of Skulls. We provide the backing at the Palais three nights a week, and the Grand Guignol for a further three. Lysander and I are gaining quite a reputation for our duets. People say that they have a quasi-competitive edge, but we're good friends, in spite of the difference in the age of our bones. Whatever one of our Larvae might once have done to the other is of no relevance to us. We're skellies; we're happy.

Jillian comes to see us perform regularly, often in company with Billy and Helen. Cleo and Hector have a meaningful relationship of their own now, and credit me with enabling them to find additional happiness together. Nurse Adelaide would probably come more frequently if she weren't intimidated by Melissa's jealous stare. Jillian isn't, and jokes about it by referring to Melissa as "Medusa"—which, unfortunately, had the unanticipated side effect of encouraging Billy to cultivate the habit of referring the pair of us as "Medusa and the Gangrene Kid." He thinks it's funny, and I try to take it in good part, although, if looks could kill, Melissa would be a multiple murderer by now.

I'm a minor celebrity of sorts among my own kind. Uncle Paulus, who fancies himself as the Chief Elder of the Skelly community, dropped into our new apartment the day I moved in to tell me that I was a credit to the osteomorphic species, and my former neighbor Jack makes a point of telling everyone that not only did he live next door to me before I was famous, but that he was the first person to see me after "the zombie attack."

I suspect that the zombie brothers still get a certain amount of abuse thrown at them even by their own kind, but I always make a point of saying hello to them and making it obvious that I don't have anything against them at all. Live and let live is my motto, even though it doesn't really apply to Postmortals, pedantically speaking, and especially not to zombies.

I haven't seen Sthenelais again after leaving the clinic, but I suspect that it's only a matter of time. I do see Dr. Charteris occasionally, though, fairly regularly. As the world's foremost expert on osteomorphic physiology, he comes into the Ghetto now and again, to consult with Dr. Setlow and other colleagues. He seems to make a point of looking me up, and although he pretends that it's some kind of check-up, I think he has some kind of hidden agenda. He even came to see me play at the Guignol once. If I ask him how his experiments Outside are going, though, he always tells me that he can't discuss it because of patient confidentiality.

Actually, I suspect that I was right about him being smart enough to figure out that the Faculty was manipulating him, and maybe even smart enough to play them at their own game. Maybe some day he'll let me in on the state of play, but for the time being, he's playing his cards close to his squishy chest. I really shouldn't care about that, and I wish I didn't, but now that I know that I have a convoluted mind, I can't help feeling a little bit curious . . . or more than a little bit, if you want the truth. Still, I'm happy. What more could any reasonable person want than that?

According to Phil, the increase in the Postmortal population in proportion to the Larval population is still alarming the Larvae, and he's heard rumors that construction will begin on a third Ghetto any day now, in the hope of staying ahead of the trend for a decade or two. There isn't much talk about it in the Ghetto, though, although the Lycanthropic Separatists seem to be increasing their support, as well as the Banish the Zombies party. It's already been decided, though, that the Australian Ghetto will have a mixed population, just like ours, taking at least ninety per cent of all new Postmortals.

I can't help wondering whether the Larvae have buried a hydrogen bomb under that one too—assuming, that is, that they really have put one under ours. But even if I am living on top of a hydrogen bomb, there's no point in worrying about it, is there? Afterlife is for living, not for fretting. After all, when you think about all the Postmortals who don't make it through death, and those who do only to find out they're zombies, there's a great deal to be said for being a skelly, and every day is precious, as long as you can be happy, and can dance. I can.

In any case, if the Larvae ever thought that it would be a good idea to detonate that bomb, it would probably turn out to be a dud. After all, you know what they say about the best laid plans . . .

A PARTIAL LIST OF SNUGGLY BOOKS